THE ADVENTURES OF RADISSON 1

HELL NEVER BURNS

Martin Fournier

THE ADVENTURES OF RADISSON 1

HELL NEVER BURNS

Translated by Peter McCambridge

Baraka
Books
Montreal

Originally published as *Les aventures de Radisson, 1 L'enfer ne brûle pas*
© 2011 by Les éditions du Septentrion
Publié avec l'autorisation de Les éditions du Septentrion, Sillery, Québec

Translation Copyright © Baraka Books 2012

Cover illustration by Jean-Michel Girard
Cover by Folio infographie
Back cover photo, Robin Philpot
Book design by Folio infographie
Translated by Peter McCambridge

Legal Deposit, 4th quarter, 2012

Bibliothèque et Archives nationales du Québec
Library and Archives Canada

Published by Baraka Books of Montreal.
6977, rue Lacroix
Montréal, Québec H4E 2V4
Telephone: 514 808-8504
info@barakabooks.com
www.barakabooks.com

Printed and bound in Quebec

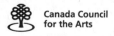

Baraka Books acknowledges the generous support of its publishing program from the Société de développement des entreprises culturelles du Québec (SODEC) and the Canada Council for the Arts.

Canada Council for the Arts

We acknowledge the financial support of the Government of Canada, through the National Translation Program for Book Publishing for our transla tion activities.

Trade Distribution & Returns
Canada
LitDistCo
1-800-591-6250
ordering@litdistco.ca

United States
Independent Publishers Group
1-800-888-4741
orders@ipgbook.com

TABLE OF CONTENTS

RADISSON'S TRAVELS AS A CAPTIVE AND AS AN IROQUOIS

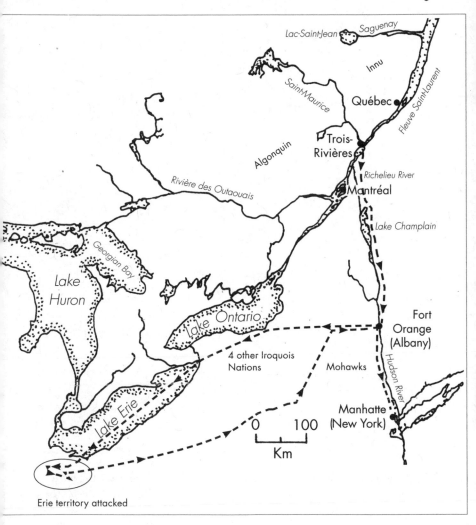

Translator's note: "In the early part of the seventeenth century the native people of Canada were not known to the French as 'Indians,' but by the names of their tribal confederacies, and were referred to collectively as 'Les Sauvages' (the Savages). The natives, for their part, spoke of the French as 'Normans' and of the Jesuit fathers as 'Blackrobes.'" – Brian Moore, from the Author's Note to *Black Robe* (Penguin: 1985), p. viii. After discussion with the historian and author of *Les aventures de Radisson*, Martin Fournier, the translator has used the term 'Wildmen' occasionally in the narrative itself, since this is the term Radisson himself used in his English-language travel journals. In the 17th century, the French term *sauvages* did not have the pejorative meaning it does today.

PIERRE-ESPRIT RADISSON IMMIGRATES TO CANADA

PIERRE-ESPRIT RADISSON was the most famous *coureur des bois* in the history of Canada. Happily, the detailed accounts he left behind give us a good idea of his extraordinary adventures.

On May 24, 1651, he left his native France at age fifteen for New France, undertaking the perilous crossing of the Atlantic from Paris to join his two sisters, Marguerite and Françoise, in Trois-Rivières. At the time, no more than three hundred lived in the village. Montréal had been founded nine years earlier and was home to less than two hundred people. Québec was the biggest settlement with over one thousand inhabitants. In all, barely two thousand French settlers lived in New France.

Trois-Rivières lay at the confluence of the Saint-Maurice and St. Lawrence rivers, a long-established meeting place for the Wildmen in summer. The French village had some thirty axe-hewn square-timber buildings surrounded by a high stockade and protected by four solid corner bastions. Only the residence of the Jesuit missionaries was built from stone. When Radisson joined his two sisters there, war was raging between the French and the powerful Iroquois nation. The

Iroquois had decimated the Hurons—their long-time enemies—the previous year. Since the Hurons were the main allies of the French in the fur trade—the colony's only source of revenue—those were critical days for New France. Its very existence was in peril.

At that time, news travelled very slowly: Radisson knew nothing of the impending crisis when he left France. Judging by the three letters his sister Marguerite had sent to her family over a period of five years, New France was a land of milk and honey. And so Radisson decided to leave his life in Paris, where he lived with his mother as a small-time trader. New France beckoned.

Radisson was astonished by all that he found in the colony: endless forests, broad expanses of water as far as the eye could see, phenomenal quantities of snow, and winters longer and colder than he could ever have imagined. Trois-Rivières was also much smaller and more isolated than he anticipated. Worse, the colony had almost come to a standstill. Radisson took up residence with his sister Marguerite and her husband Jean Véron dit Grandmesnil. But he soon had enough of being shut up inside the village.

||||||||||||||||||||||||||||||||||||||||||||||||||||||||||||||||||||||||||||||||||||||||||||||||||||||||

CHAPTER 1

RADISSON KNOWS NO FEAR

E YES BURSTING with energy, mouth stuffed full of moose, head spinning with the thirst for life that devoured him, Radisson found it hard to pay attention as his brother-in-law Jean Véron retold his favourite story for the twentieth time.

"You should've seen our twelve canoes weighted down with all those furs!" he roared. "When we got within sight of Trois-Rivières, with Saint-Claude and the three Huron chiefs in the first canoe, I was so happy I fired my musket into the air! Everyone ran out to the shore to meet us. We beached the canoes, climbed out, and hugged each other heartily. The men couldn't believe all the fur we brought back and my beautiful Marguerite kissed me all over, tears of joy streaming down her face..."

Radisson pictured himself travelling the length and breadth of the endless expanses he'd heard about from the men who'd returned from the lands to the west. He dreamed of reaching the ends of the earth, and finding great riches and happiness. He felt prepared for adventure.

"The Jesuit missionaries who had come back with us embraced those who stayed behind. Then Father Le Mercier, the Superior, thanked the Hurons for once again coming from so far to trade their furs, despite the dangers of the journey.

They'd be more than happy with what the French would give them in exchange, he promised. Then we sat down and the feasting began. Our beaver pelts turned more heads than even the *eau-de-vie*..."

Outside a ferocious snowstorm was beating down on the tiny settlement of Trois-Rivières. Radisson had never seen anything like it. From time to time he paused between mouthfuls to listen to the jets of snow rattling against the windowpanes like sand thrown by a giant hand. With each terrible gust of wind the fire flared up, swallowing the logs Marguerite kept feeding the hearth to fight off the cold. The wind blew through the village, howled in the woods, veered out over the frozen St. Lawrence as the snow piled up around the houses as they struggled to resist the storm and cling to their heat, huddled tight up against one another, protected by the stockade that blunted the worst of the icy squalls. Noticing that his sister and brother-in-law seemed unconcerned, Radisson went on eating.

"That's the trade that made us rich," Véron continued. "Not as rich as the merchants in Québec now, not that rich! But for people like us, here in Trois-Rivières we can't complain, can we, Marguerite? Can't complain at all! From that day on the governor of Québec has had complete confidence in me—even writes to me for advice!"

Marguerite had finished tidying the kitchen. Carefully she cast another log onto the hearth through the flames, and then sat down with her husband and Radisson at the table. Her belly had begun to swell with the child that would be born in the summer. Seeing that her brother was devouring her moose stew, she asked, "Another plate, Radisson? It sure looks like you're enjoying it!"

Radisson nodded enthusiastically, a smile dancing across his lips, delighted to discover meat he had never tasted before.

Back from their great winter hunt, the Algonquins who lived no more than fifty feet away from the fort had traded some to Véron and Marguerite in return for flour and peas. Radisson had never heard of the Algonquins before, but he soon learned they were indispensable allies of the French against the Iroquois. Like everyone who lived in Trois-Rivières, he encountered them nearly every day. Their complicated language, the clothing they made from animal skins, and their strange ways all fascinated him.

Jean Véron finished his story. He fell silent for a moment, lost in thought, then changed tone and turned to his wife.

"Ah Marguerite, those were the days," he sighed.

"Don't worry, my love. They'll return soon enough," she replied. "Trade will pick up again, just like before. It's only a bad patch."

"From your mouth to God's ear, woman! If things keep on like this, it'll be the end of trade in the Great Lakes! As long as the Iroquois are at war with us, we won't be going back there in a hurry, that's for sure."

Gloomily Jean Véron returned to his thoughts, as though talk of the war against the Iroquois had robbed him of his voice, his hope. Meanwhile Radisson finished off his stew without batting an eyelid. The whole household could hear him slurping away each time the wind died down and the crackling of the fire subsided. He had never seen an Iroquois in his life and didn't understand the gravity of the situation. Marguerite put a firm, reassuring hand on her husband's shoulder and some of his energy returned. He looked at Radisson again:

"Lads like you are going to help us get through," he said. "When spring comes, you'll come to Québec with me to take orders from the governor. Then, if you like, you'll come to Montréal with the men who are prepared to go with us and we'll find a way to resist the Iroquois and, above all else, replace the Hurons and find new trading partners for our furs. We can't give up, lad. The colony may be collapsing around us, but we have to pick ourselves back up! We have to fight! Otherwise everyone is going to run off back to France. Is that what you want, lad? To run right back where you came from? No, eh? Well, then you'll do your bit! I bet you're all set to help us. What do you think, Marguerite?"

"Of course my brother's going to help!" she said confidently. "I'd even go so far as to say that he wants nothing more than to help us. Isn't that right, Radisson?"

"That's for sure!" the young Frenchman exclaimed, nodding emphatically, his mouth still full of the bread he'd sopped up the gravy with.

PIERRE GODEFROY, the most experienced man in all of Trois-Rivières, had just been chosen by the *habitants* to captain the militia. From then on, he would lead the fight against the Iroquois. For fifteen years he'd travelled everywhere with the Indians; he knew their languages, their ruses and customs. Like them, he knew how to hunt, fish, repair a canoe, and find his way through the woods. He knew the ways of the animals, the wild plants that healed and nourished, and the dangers that winter and spring could bring. He was tall, strapping, and strong as an ox, with hands as broad as paddles. Around him he gathered all the men who could bear arms outside the fort, within sight of the Saint-Maurice and St. Lawrence rivers. Speaking for the first time as captain, he addressed them in a booming voice. The three officers of the militia, his assistants, stood by his side.

Radisson was one of the youngest members in the group, along with his friend François Godefroy—the captain's son—

and Mathurin Lesueur, a beanpole of a lad who'd arrived in Trois-Rivières a few weeks after Radisson the previous summer.

Instead of listening to Pierre Godefroy, Radisson let his eyes wander to the bright horizon. He could see exactly the passageway, along the St. Lawrence, to the far-off lands he dreamed of. The bright sunshine warmed his face. Spring was in the air, his friend François told him. Even though Paris was already warm at this time of year, Radisson couldn't have been happier to be in New France, a good distance from the village stockade that no longer blocked his gaze, or curbed his imagination. Here he was, happy to stare off into the wide-open spaces that beckoned to him irresistibly.

"The Iroquois are bound to attack us," said Godefroy. "So we will have to ready ourselves. We have nothing to fear so long as we fight together. That's why it's vital to do what I and my officers tell you."

Looking toward the steeple atop the Jesuit chapel and the smoking chimneys that peeked above the stockade, Radisson told himself that he was an apprentice no more. No more comments about his lack of experience and the country's many dangers. Soon it would be his turn to step out into the world. He was ready.

"You know your officers as well as I do," Godefroy continued. "I have appointed Jean Véron dit Grandmesnil..."

Radisson's ears pricked up at the sound of his brother-in-law's name. How proud he was that his sister's husband had been named first officer of the militia after Godefroy. Véron had taught him how to fire a musket, an unthinkable privilege in France for anyone not a soldier or a nobleman.

"...Claude Volant dit Saint-Claude," shouted Godefroy, "and Gabriel Dandonneau. These will be my three right-hand men. But we're also counting on each and every one of you! From now on you will go on daily patrols around the fort, in groups of five or six in Indian file. And you will practice your shooting. Radisson. Come here!"

The young Frenchman couldn't believe his ears. He didn't dare move. Why was Godefroy calling him forward? What had he done wrong, especially now that he was listening to the captain's every word?

"Radisson!" Godefroy shouted again. "Come here, I said!"

His friend François motioned for him to step forward and be quick about it. Radisson walked over to his captain, impressed by the strength that emanated from his broad belly.

"Stand here," Godefroy told him. "Show them how to shoot. Now listen: when I throw this piece of wood up into the air and shout 'Fire!' you open fire. Got it?"

"Yes, sir," replied Radisson.

A lump in his throat, legs slightly bent for greater balance, feet planted firmly on his snowshoes, and musket level with his chest, Radisson steadied himself. He was keen to make a good impression, to prove that he deserved the trust Godefroy had placed in him. Suddenly Godefroy threw the wood high into the air and yelled "Fire!" Radisson brought the musket to his shoulder, aimed, pulled the trigger, and hit the branch. It tumbled through the air. "I hit it! I hit it!" shouted Radisson, hoisting his arms and turning toward the men looking on, the delight on his face clear for all to see.

"See that?" said Godefroy. "I wanted to show you that you don't need to be a soldier to be a good shot. Radisson never even held a gun before he came over here. But he's worked hard and he's learned well. In just six months, he's better with a musket than many of you. You can do anything if you set your minds to it. Now, if you all do the exercises I give you, you'll only get better and we'll have nothing to fear from the Iroquois! We will be stronger than anyone."

Radisson was still thrilled and surprised at having shown everyone he was one of the sharpest shooters in Trois-Rivières. One man after another came up to congratulate him and pass on words of encouragement, aware that they needed young recruits like him if they were to regain the upper hand in the war against the Iroquois. He thanked them with his finest smile; he'd always found it easy to get on well with people. In Paris he'd already discovered the benefits of serving his father's customers with enthusiasm and good humour: it loosened their purse strings and kept them coming back.

"Follow me, now!" ordered Pierre Godefroy. "Everybody run!"

His triumph still fresh in everyone's mind, Radisson was keen to again prove that he was one of the best. He rushed forward but, unused to running on snowshoes, fell headfirst into the snow. François didn't miss the chance to exact his revenge:

"Ah, now we can all see the new guys aren't up to much," he said scornfully. "You can't always be lucky like earlier, can you?"

"Shut up, François Godefroy. You know I'm a better shot than you!" replied Radisson as he struggled to get up, tangled in his snowshoes. "Give me a hand, will you?"

But François ran on ahead without turning round, in high spirits. Radisson caught up with him a few minutes later at the Algonquin camp. His father had already begun to address their chief in the Algonquin language. Radisson could barely understand a word. He leaned over to his friend, who spoke the language fluently, and whispered, "What's your dad saying?"

François was only too happy to show he knew more than Radisson and whispered back: "He is sorry so many Algonquins died when the Iroquois attacked them four years ago. He says that the French have come in force to pledge to fight alongside them and prevent another massacre. He wants to know if the Algonquins will agree to fight with the French."

Radisson was very impressed by the chief, who expressed himself nobly, weighing each of his words as though he had an important secret to share. He asked François to translate but Jean Véron, who was standing beside them, motioned for them to be quiet. Radisson managed to grasp only a few words: "summer... Saint-Maurice River... alliance... many brothers... my word..." As soon as Godefroy brought the meeting to a close by ordering a return to the fort, Radisson again asked François to translate the Algonquin chief's reply.

"I can't remember," replied François.

"I don't believe you," said Radisson. "Tell me, please tell me, François. Give it a try."

"I don't feel like it."

"You have to teach me Algonquin, François! I want to learn Algonquin. Say something in Algonquin, anything at all. Talk to me, I'm listening."

Springtime had come at last. Ever since the ice on the St. Lawrence gave way with an almighty crack one night in April, Radisson felt a fever building up inside him. Every day he pestered Jean Véron about when they would be leaving for Québec, as he'd promised. At the very least he yearned to get out of the fort to hunt the Canada geese that filled the skies. It drove him wild to see the geese flying over the village and landing on the St. Lawrence in their thousands, just beyond the stockade, where they fed, then flew off again only to be replaced by still more.

But instead of seizing the chance to feast on such an abundance of fresh meat after Lent—which the Jesuits had seen was observed to the letter—Pierre Godefroy ordered everyone to remain in the village until further notice. He had heard from a settler from Montréal that the Iroquois were back. Apart from Godefroy, nobody in Trois-Rivières believed a word of it, since the Iroquois had never before arrived so early in the season. But for the captain of the militia, this was no time for taking risks. Radisson wouldn't have minded if they had gone to Québec immediately to get their orders from the governor. But they hadn't moved. Everything was at a standstill: no hunting, no travelling to Québec, nothing. Jean Véron was tying himself in knots, putting off the trip for one unlikely reason after another. Radisson would have done anything to put an end to the standstill that was eating away at him.

One morning, to his great surprise, he saw that Jean Véron was nowhere to be found. "Where did he go?" he asked his sister, apprehensively. At first Marguerite didn't dare tell him the secret she'd been reluctantly guarding for the past few days. Then she gave in: her husband had left by canoe during the night with Pierre Godefroy and Claude Volant to meet the governor in Québec. They'd decided to leave alone in secret for reasons of safety, she explained. Radisson exploded with rage.

"Liar!" he shouted, slamming his fist down on the table. "He's a damned liar! He promised he'd take me with him."

Marguerite tried to calm her brother.

"There was no choice, Radisson. We have to be more careful than ever. The Iroquois have already killed enough of us as it is. Pierre and Jean didn't want to take any risks. They kept the whole thing a secret."

"I'm stronger than any of them, you'll see!" said Radisson, not listening. "If they'd taken me with them, we'd already be in Québec by now!"

"It takes more than strength to paddle," Marguerite replied calmly. "You've hardly even been in a canoe, Radisson. You don't know the first thing about it. It's not as easy as it looks."

"How am I going to learn when nobody wants to show me? All I want is to learn to paddle. Like I learned to shoot. At least give me a chance! But oh no, it's always the same old story: wait your turn, lad, you're not old enough yet. Véron is a damned liar! What kind of life is this? If I could at least go hunting! Tell me why we're not allowed to hunt? Nobody believes the Iroquois are here! Somebody's messing with us!"

"It's safer that way," Marguerite replied, but without much conviction.

Far from convinced the Iroquois were an imminent threat, she looked for a way to cheer her brother up. He was moping more and more with every passing day.

"Perhaps you could go hunting just opposite the fort with your friends," she suggested. "There are so many geese! You're bound to hit three or four of them. And I can't wait to eat fresh meat..."

Her offer had an immediate effect on Radisson, who jumped to his feet, full of enthusiasm.

"Seriously?" he cried, raring to go. "Can I really?"

"Why not? I think Jean would agree. As long as you stay within sight of the fort and François and your friends go with you. You're well armed and not too far away—you should be fine."

"Great idea! I'll run and see if François is game. I'll be back right away."

Radisson dashed outside like the wind. His first stop was at Mathurin Lesueur's house. Even though he found him a little dull and rather awkward, Radisson had made him his friend since they were both the same age. There were so few young people in Trois-Rivières. Radisson quickly told him about his sister's plan.

"Marguerite says we can go hunting opposite the fort," he told him. "She wants us to bring back enough for everyone! Your mom is going to be so happy, Mathurin. Get ready and I'll go find François. See you in a minute!"

But Radisson had more trouble convincing François Godefroy.

"My dad says we're not allowed out of the fort," he said, confidently. "There's no way I'm going. It's not your sister that calls the shots around here, or her husband—it's my dad."

"It's for the common good, François!" argued Radisson, using his full powers of persuasion. Everybody's tired of eating rotten turnips, tasteless onions, and salt pork. Just listen to the geese! They're calling to us, all day long! They *want* us to come feast on them! Have you ever heard of someone turning up his nose at what God has been good enough to send him every spring? It's practically a sin, staying here instead of going out hunting!"

"Our safety is at stake," countered François. "All my dad wants is to keep us safe from the Iroquois."

"Maybe. But who ever saw an Iroquois round here in early May? No one. Nobody believes the garbage that guy from Montréal was spouting! The Iroquois are doing exactly what we should be doing, François—they're out hunting geese while they're still around! It'll soon be too late. There's nothing to worry about—we won't be far. We'll stay opposite the fort. The guards will see us from the palisade. Marguerite has been living here five years, you know! And your dad made Véron, her husband, first officer of the militia. My sister knows what she's talking about. Come on, François! Mathurin and I are going anyway. But you're the one with all the experience, and you're a better hunter than we are. Come on, François. It's for the common good…"

At that moment, a flock of geese flew just over their heads in a V, filling the bright, clear sky with their cackling. François' mouth watered at the thought of all the tasty roast goose he'd ever eaten. His resistance weakened.

"My brother Jacques did leave this morning with the Algonquins to go up the Saint-Maurice River…"

"You see! Anyway, all the officers have gone except Dandonneau. Nobody will be angry we went hunting. No way! Your own mom will be thanking you for bringing fresh meat home. Come on, François—we're going!"

"Fine. I'm in as long as we stay within sight of the fort. We'll be safe if we do that. We'll kill a goose or two each and then come back."

"Great!"

Radisson was over the moon. He'd done it! At last he would be able to get outside and make himself useful. Marguerite would have preferred there be more of them, but she trusted the three, especially with the experienced François, and didn't go back on her word. Radisson put his greased moccasins on as fast as he could, then picked up his musket, powder horn, and pouches of lead shot. It was a perfect day for hunting: warm and sunny. Radisson was wearing only a linen shirt and pants. Marguerite watched him get ready without saying a word, delighted to see him back in high spirits after so much disappointment. She gave him only one piece of advice:

"Whatever you do, don't go wandering off from the fort. That's what we agreed. Just be patient, little brother. You're sure to bring back plenty of geese."

"Don't worry. You can start getting your pots ready. I promise you we're going to have a real feast tonight!"

"Here, take a loaf with you," added Marguerite, handing him a big hunk of fresh bread. "It'll keep you going all day."

Radisson stuffed it into his shoulder bag and left the house, but an idea flashed before him and he went back to take Véron's musket from above the hearth, in addition to his own.

"I'm borrowing your husband's musket," he explained. "He owes me that at least. Two muskets will mean more geese for everyone. See you later!"

Marguerite was only too happy to have solved the problem. The hunting would do her little brother good: he really was beginning to get fidgety feet. "Just so he doesn't stray too far," she thought.

THE GUARD keeping watch over the fort's main gate at first refused to let the three young men through. They reminded him of the need to bring back fresh food, orders or no orders. To convince him, they promised to bring him back the fourth goose they shot, if fortune smiled on them, that is. The guard didn't believe the Iroquois would have come so early in the season and would have liked nothing more than to go hunting himself, so he let them pass. "Provided you stay close by and don't tell anyone it was me who let you out."

The three companions left the village, crying out with springtime glee. Radisson felt as free as the geese flying overhead. In a few hours, he'd be bringing a mouth-watering meal back to Marguerite and would give some of the meat to his sister Françoise who worked for the Jesuits. Everyone would be happy and proud of him.

In no time at all they reached the edge of the meadow that surrounded the village, heading for the St. Lawrence. Undergrowth separated them from the shore, which was further away than it looked. It took them a few minutes more to reach the last thickets, just steps away from the riverbank. What better place to surprise the geese, even though, for the moment, they were all still too far away. All they had to do was wait... wait... and wait some more... Staying still for so long quickly began to grate on Radisson's nerves.

After an hour, not a single bird had come within musket range. Radisson could make out a huge white patch of thousands of geese out on the water, much further away. "All the geese are over there," he argued. "We'll have to flush them out. There's no point waiting around here."

François and Mathurin didn't agree. They'd given their word to stay within sight of the fort. But they finally gave in to their friend. The three of them started walking along the shoreline. Soon the palisade of Trois-Rivières was nothing more than a faint line above the brushwood. Young vivid green leaves masked their surroundings. The three companions could now see only a short distance in front of them. Soon it became clear that no one would be able to see them from Trois-Rivières.

"Hey! We've lost sight of the village!" protested Mathurin. "We said we wouldn't go far. We'll have to go back."

"Chicken!" replied Radisson, without even turning round. "We're almost there. In fifteen minutes we'll have bagged two or three geese each and be on our way back. Come on!"

Mathurin stopped for a moment, looking carefully around him. He would have liked to see the reassuring sight of the palisade, but it had disappeared. Fear took hold of his stomach. Even the bushes seemed threatening; he thought he could see Iroquois hiding all around him. But Radisson and François were already in the marsh grass, on their way to the river. Reluctantly, Mathurin ran to catch up with them, scared of being alone. The three made slow progress through deeper and deeper water, crouching down so as not to scare the geese. Mathurin couldn't help showing his distress once more: "It's dangerous," he managed to stutter, his voice trembling.

"Shut up!" Radisson retorted. He was leading the way, and stood up straight to face Mathurin. "You're going to scare the geese!"

At the same time, a first goose took flight in the distance, then another, then ten, then a hundred, then a thousand all at once! A whole white cloud of them swelled, banked, then pitched to the west in one exquisite movement. Radisson ran in their direction, took aim, and fired... But they were too far away. Their highly coveted prey remained beyond their reach. François didn't even bother firing. Radisson turned round angrily and upbraided Mathurin: "It's your fault! If you hadn't said anything, we'd have been close enough to get at them!"

"You're the one who shouted!" retorted Mathurin. "It's your fault! You don't even know how to hunt! I'm not taking lessons from you!"

The two friends pushed and shoved each other for a moment. François stayed to one side. He was the only experienced hunter among them and he knew that patience was the key—a quality that Radisson still lacked. When peace reigned once again between the two companions, he asked them to walk back to within sight of the fort and work out what to do next. When Trois-Rivières was once again close by, Radisson again convinced them to return to where the geese were. And so they headed westward again, this time following François' lead, which meant walking across the cleared fields tilled by the rare farmers who lived outside the Trois-Rivières stockade, a route that François believed would be safer.

No sooner had they gotten close to the first farm house than a man shouted out to them from inside the building: "Halt!" A middle-aged *habitant* with a stoop unbolted his door and came out carrying a musket. "You young 'uns are all mad! The Iroquois are out in droves—you're going to get yourselves massacred! Now clear off before I fill your hides full of lead!"

The threat set the three lads back on their heels: now they didn't know what to think. But François recognized the farmer and remembered that he had a bad reputation: it was Old Man Bouchard, who sold alcohol to the Wildmen, even though the Jesuits didn't allow it. And he didn't seem to be all there. Mathurin, who was already scared stiff, believed every word he said, but François wondered if he'd been drinking and wanted to see if what he was saying really made sense.

"Where did you see them then?" he asked.

"Down by the river," replied Bouchard, pointing to the water. "Right down there at the far end of my field!"

Radisson stared into the distance, even less convinced than François.

"Sure you can see that far, old man?" he asked arrogantly.

"Dead right I can, boy! No mistaking an Iroquois. Saw a hundred of them, I did. With feathers sticking out of their heads. Now get back home before they eat you up for dinner!"

"We're going, we're going," said Mathurin, his voice shaking.

"Over there?" Radisson asked. "Right where I can see the Bogeyman?"

"Go to hell, you little brat! Too bad for you if they scalp you. I warned you. Now goodnight all!"

And with that the farmer disappeared back into his house just as quickly as he'd come out. They could hear him sliding the bar back across his door. Two seconds later his worried face reappeared in the tiny window overlooking the St. Lawrence. He was still holding his fowling piece.

"If you ask me, we should go look for footprints," suggested François. "May as well be clear about it in our own minds. If they are here, we'll go warn Dandonneau right away. Muskets at the ready, lads. We need to be careful."

"Oh, no!" Mathurin sighed.

Once they reached the edge of the forest separating the cleared field from the river, the young adventurers peered long and hard into the bushes, then inspected the ground for footprints. They listened to the wind whistling through the branches, the cracks of vegetation, and the far-off cackling of wildfowl. Nothing appeared to be out of place.

"We'll keep going as far as the river," announced Radisson, walking deeper into the woods.

Ready for anything, they moved slowly from one tree to another. Terrified, Mathurin fell behind, following his companions reluctantly, shaking. Radisson and François motioned to each other. They pointed out a tree, a grove, or a shadow, and covered each other. Fifty feet further on, when they at last reached the shoreline, Radisson let his guard down: "See? No Iroquois here. The old fool was wrong!" François, who was less certain, continued to scan the ground, searching apprehensively for the slightest evidence that would confirm his intuition.

"Just because we haven't seen any Iroquois doesn't mean they're not here," he said at last. "They're masters of concealment."

"Whatever," Radisson replied. "They're not ghosts, you know—just Iroquois!"

"That shows you don't know them," François answered, continuing to examine their surroundings, as though he felt like he was being spied on. "There's nothing more cunning than an Iroquois. You'd better learn that quickly or you won't last long in New France."

"Perhaps. But at the minute all I see is thousands of geese right over there. Follow me! This time we're not going to miss out!"

"No way!" said François. "I'm going back to Trois-Rivières. We've already gone much further than we wanted to. It's dangerous out here. We need to warn Dandonneau that Old Bouchard has seen Iroquois."

"Is there something wrong with your head?" Radisson was starting to lose his temper. "We have no more than a hundred paces to go and then we can kill as many geese as we like. Old Bouchard is half mad. We haven't seen the slightest trace of any Iroquois. And you want to go running back to your mommy?

You're nothing but a chicken, François Godefroy! I promised Marguerite I would bring back goose for tonight's dinner and by God that's exactly what I'm going to do! So long, scaredy-cats! Get yourselves laughed at, if you like. I'm going on."

Radisson turned on his heels and moved rapidly toward the geese, bent over so as not to scare them again. Mathurin couldn't wait to get back to the fort, but François hesitated for a long while, his teeth clenched and his pride wounded. Finally he decided that he was duty bound to return to the fort and warn Dandonneau, and headed back toward Trois-Rivières.

"Let's go," he whispered to Mathurin. "We'll go back along the shore. If we're lucky, we'll run into the geese along the way."

It took Radisson a few minutes to reach the geese he'd thought were much closer. Thousands of geese and ducks were resting nonchalantly in the middle of a huge expanse of partially submerged bulrushes. He walked slowly toward them, bent double, so as not to frighten them away. The cold water rushed into his moccasins and was soon up to his knees. He kept going, careful to keep the powder in his shoulder bag dry. His second musket was slung across his shoulder, hampering his progress, but he was glad he had brought it. He'd be able to shoot twice each time and bag more birds.

The geese were nervous; Radisson knew they'd take off at the slightest movement. As soon as he reckoned he was close enough to be sure of hitting the target, he stopped, took aim, and fired a first time. Hundreds of frightened birds flapped their wings in panic, scooping frantically at the water with their feet as they took to the air, all crying out at once. Radisson grabbed his other musket, aimed, and fired a second time. A handful of birds fell from a sky now black and white and brown with them. A deafening racket of straining wings, anguished cackles, and whipped-up water filled the air. The immense flock took flight, pirouetted, and scattered itself overhead. Some of the geese landed much further away, but masses of them rose higher and higher in the sky, lost for good. Radisson stood gaping at the dazzling spectacle and took a moment or two to find his bearings. Now all he had to do was collect the dozen or so dead geese floating not too far away. He waded further out until he was knee deep in water, trying hard to keep his shoulder bag and muskets dry. It was hard going, hauling the geese one by one back to shore. He managed to pile up seven of them, nice and dry on a little mound of sand. Then, without warning, cold and fatigue assailed him. Radisson had to sit down and rest for a long while, leaving his muskets to dry in the sun. Despite his precautions the butts were soaked, but the firing mechanisms and barrels were still dry. He devoured the bread Marguerite gave him. The food made him feel better, but it couldn't drive away the concern that was beginning to gnaw at him. He had strayed much too far. Here he was, all alone, making enough noise to draw any number of Iroquois who might have happened to be in the neighbourhood. He hoped that François was wrong about them, that his father, the man from Montréal, and Old Bouchard were all wrong too... otherwise he could be in real trouble.

Radisson managed to keep calm and get his bearings. Judging by the sun, it must have been two o'clock in the afternoon and he was about three hours from Trois-Rivières. He was reassured at the thought that he'd be able to make it back home by nightfall, even before the evening Angelus if he got a move on. First, though, he reloaded his muskets just to be sure, checking that the powder was still dry. After carefully tamping the powder well down into the barrel he slid in the lead shot and the piece of wadding that kept everything in place. He picked up Jean Véron's weapon and filled it with six medium-sized shots that would be sure to injure any assailants he might encounter and send them packing. He put his biggest lead shot into his own, to kill if need be.

Radisson's pants and moccasins were still soaked, but the sun was beating down; he began to warm up a bit as the cold started to fade. He felt ready to set off on the long way home. But the seven geese were dreadfully heavy and burdensome; he didn't quite know how he was going to carry them. His shoulder bag wouldn't be enough. After thinking it over for a while, he came up with an ingenious solution. After winding the strap of his bag around the long necks of his catch, he threw the bag over his shoulder, three birds behind him and three in front. Then he slung Jean Véron's gun over his free shoulder and grabbed the seventh goose by the neck with his left hand, carrying his own musket in his right hand. It was heavy, but he could just about manage. His feet dragging, Radisson headed straight along the shoreline, avoiding the obstacle-filled woods that would only slow him down. The walk would be long and tiring, but he was determined to bring his haul home with him, all of it.

After an hour, Radisson was exhausted. "These geese weigh a ton!" he groaned. He stopped to drink clear, fresh water from the river and rest for a moment. Barely had he refreshed himself when he sensed a presence behind him. He whirled around like lightning—but there was no one to be seen. And yet he still felt danger tying his stomach in knots. Radisson picked up his firearms and geese and broke into a run. He dashed headlong into the woods, took a few strides, and then abruptly crouched down, not moving, hardly breathing, nervous, alert to everything around him. But he heard only the wind in the trees, the birds singing, and the pounding of his heart ... not the slightest sound to draw his suspicion. He tried to calm himself. In vain. "I'm tired," he thought. Images of grimacing Iroquois descended upon him, like flies over a corpse. He must be going mad, he thought; death was shrieking in his ears. He couldn't take it any longer, left everything right where it was, and crawled away with one musket. He tracked back on himself in a roundabout way, hiding opposite the geese tied up to his shoulder bag, beside Jean Véron's gun, which he'd left at the foot of a tall tree. "If the Iroquois are about," he said to himself, "they're going to come for my spoils." Then, all he'd have to do was run for his life.

But nothing happened. For what seemed forever, Radisson froze. Nobody came. He shook his head with all his strength to chase away the bad thoughts that were tormenting him. At last he got back on his feet and went to pick up his geese. He knew he had to make tracks if he wanted to reach Trois-Rivières by nightfall. Nothing could stand in his way. He swallowed the last of his bread and retraced his steps back to the riverbank with his heavy load, then headed quickly along the shore.

Time flew by without him noticing. He tried his best not to think of anything at all. Just walk as fast as he could. He thought of Marguerite, all the same, and her bright idea of giving him bread for the day. "God bless you, dear sister," he thought. He felt annoyed at himself for breaking their agreement. "Just so you stay within sight of the fort and François and your friends go with you," he heard her saying to him again and again, as it sank in just how reckless he'd been. But his ordeal was nearing an end: he recognized the spot where he left his companions. Suddenly he felt much calmer. He promised to give a goose each to François, Mathurin, and the guard that let them out to make amends. There was plenty of meat for everyone. He'd give two to his sister Françoise for the Jesuits, and that would leave two for him and Marguerite. To hell with Jean Véron if there was none left by the time he got back! Too bad for him. Everyone would be happy. All's well that ends well. He'd learn from this...

It was then that Radisson spotted two strange shapes lying a little to his left in the long grass. They were not tree trunks, nor animal carcasses. He feared he knew what they were but disbelieving, walked up to... the horribly mutilated, arrow-riddled bodies of François and Mathurin! Horrified, terrorized, he flung his load to the ground and recoiled. He felt sick at the sight of their blood-soaked bodies lacerated from head to toe, their disfigured faces oozing blood. He vomited hard. But he couldn't take his eyes off their scalped heads, their hair cut sliced from their foreheads then torn off, their bodies slashed with knife wounds, carved up like animals. "Why didn't they fight back?" he wondered, horrified. "Why didn't I hear anything? There's no way..." Radisson refused to see the truth, but there was no denying their grimacing faces, covered in still warm blood, no denying their still soft flesh.

A violent shiver ran through his body. Radisson could feel death closing in on him, cruel and ruthless. Instinctively, he fired into the air to alert the people of Trois-Rivières, so they could come to his aid. But it was a forlorn hope from so far away. And now he had only one shot left. He pointed his other musket aimlessly in front of him, ready to defend himself at all costs. And then, just like that, he saw ten Iroquois with brightly painted faces half hiding in the bushes! He took aim and was about to fire when terrible screams from behind him made his blood run cold. He turned around and saw twenty Iroquois warriors racing toward him. He fired blindly at the powerful bodies as they overpowered him. Their cries and their weapons beat down upon him. Radisson tried to put up a fight but it was impossible. The Iroquois pinned him to the ground and a violent blow to the head knocked him unconscious.

|||||||||||||||||||||||||||||||||||||||||||||||||||||||||||||||||||||||||||||||||||||||||||||||||

CHAPTER 2

BETWEEN LIFE AND DEATH

THE INTENSE PAIN awakened Radisson. It was as if his head was trying to split in two. He couldn't move: his arms and legs were tightly bound. "If it hurts," he thought, "that means I'm still alive. Thank God!" He'd been spread-eagled, naked, on the ground, ankles and wrists bound to stakes driven into the earth. The horror of his friends' mutilated bodies flashed through his mind. Suddenly overcome by intense anxiety, his breath came in gasps. A cloud of mosquitoes swarmed around him, drinking his blood in short, painful gulps. He blew at them to chase them away, but his head hurt twice as much. He resolved not to move again, waiting with resignation for his fate to be decided.

An Iroquois noticed the prisoner was awake and stepped toward him. Radisson looked on in terror as the Iroquois leaned over him. Broad black and white strokes painted across his face gave him a threatening look. His bare head, dirty and glistening, was divided into two by a short, narrow strip of hair that made him look ferocious, impenetrable. The man remained impassive for a long while, then smiled at Radisson. Was the Iroquois smiling because he was about to finish him off, Radisson wondered, or should he take some hope from the smile? The Iroquois vanished as quickly as he'd appeared.

Radisson, once again alone with his anguish, tried to understand why he wasn't executed on the spot, like his friends. He remembered what Jean Véron told him one day about the appalling ways the Iroquois tortured their prisoners: scorching burns to the skin, torn-out nerves, scalding-hot sand over the head... He was surprised to find himself envying his massacred friends and implored God to spare him such terrible punishments.

Not far away, just out of his sight, Radisson could hear the Iroquois singing, talking, and feasting in the light of the setting sun. The reflected light of a huge, crackling fire, giving off clouds of smoke danced around him. Radisson was probably unconscious for an hour or two. He must still have been close to Trois-Rivières, but it didn't seem as though the Iroquois feared retaliation from the French or the Algonquins. Guided by the fire and the chanting, anyone could easily find and attack them, but the Iroquois didn't appear to be in the least concerned. They were in control. There was more pain to come, Radisson feared. His strength abandoned him. His unforgivable mistake had sealed his fate. Suffering and death awaited him.

At the very depths of despair, he saw three well-built men approach. After cutting his bonds they lifted him up off the ground, grabbed hold of him, tied a rope around his neck, and pushed him right up to the edge of the fire. Fifty or so Iroquois greeted him with cries of delight, jostling and hitting him. To his great surprise, the Iroquois man he first saw when he woke up pushed away most of the men who wanted to beat him. The men who untied him forced him to sit on a fallen tree trunk opposite the fire. They gave Radisson a chunk of rotten meat that he couldn't bring himself to swallow, and his queasiness caused great mirth among his captors. Then the Iroquois that appeared to be on his side handed him his own piece of roasted meat and gave him something to drink. Despite the throbbing pain in his head, Radisson managed to chew and swallow a few mouthfuls and his worries receded a little. The respite didn't last long. Without wasting any time, a group of warriors bound him hand and foot and threw him into a canoe. The bloody scalps of his friends François and Mathurin hung before his eyes. Radisson couldn't stop himself from throwing up as he witnessed a portent of his own death. His captors were doing everything they could to terrorize him. Weak and demoralized, he lay prostrate against the bottom of the canoe. He closed his eyes, prepared to accept the torments his executioners were about to inflict upon him. He scarcely noticed that the whole band of Iroquois was busily paddling west, at an impressive clip.

When he opened his eyes, after a long moment of uncontrollable terror, Radisson saw, by the pale light of the full moon, the Iroquois who shown him some kindness. The Iroquois was sitting in front of him, right beside the revolting scalps of his friends. He was impressed by the warrior's muscular build and the strength with which he paddled. To allow him to move more freely, the man untied the rope from around Radisson's neck and fastened it to his waist. Despite his strength, the young Frenchman didn't feel up to battling these giants. "Where are they taking me now?" he wondered, noticing they were moving further and further away from Trois-Rivières and his chances of salvation.

At dawn the Iroquois stopped at last to set up camp at the mouth of a large river that flowed from the south, on a sandy shore perfectly suited to their needs. They beached their canoes and gathered wood for a fire. Here the band camped for three days until another group of Iroquois arrived from the west to meet them. For all of the following night, a good two hundred Iroquois celebrated their success: the other group also had prisoners, two Frenchmen. But they were kept apart and Radisson could only catch a distant glimpse of them now and again. The Iroquois danced around the fire, brandishing in triumph a dozen scalps at the end of long sticks, showing off their deathly trophies with sinister exuberance.

Over the three days of festivities Radisson slowly regained his confidence. Ganaha, the kindly Iroquois who was in a way his personal protector saw to it that he came to no harm. Though he believed his odds of survival to be slim indeed, hope again began to stir in his heart. On the morning of the fourth day, Ganaha painted half of Radisson's face red and the other half black. Then, his captors clambered back into their canoes and paddled south, along a broad river. To his great relief, the scalps of François and Mathurin had disappeared.

No MORE THAN four canoes and nineteen warriors headed back upriver. The trip went by peacefully. The Iroquois paddled strongly for days on end, making steady progress against the current. At times the river bottom was so rocky and the current so powerful that they had to drag their canoes along by rope from the shoreline to negotiate the rapids. Each time, Radisson did his share, dragging his canoe along. It didn't take long for him to understand that he would have to show goodwill if he was to escape the Iroquois' wrath. He would like to learn to paddle as efficiently as the others, he told them. After asking a few times, his keeper finally agreed to teach him how to paddle without tiring himself out. "Keep your arms straight," he gestured. "Put the paddle into the water in front of you and push with your chest and shoulders to propel it behind you." Once again, Radisson proved to be a good student and a fast learner. Ganaha was clearly pleased at the progress shown by his prisoner, who was happy to forget his sad fate for a moment.

Without knowing it, Radisson was saving his life. The decision to execute or spare him lay in the hands of Ganaha, who chose to capture rather than kill him after Radisson left François and Mathurin to continue his hunting expedition alone. Ganaha and his brother Ongienda followed him from afar to judge his worth. His audacity impressed Ganaha. The Iroquois brave could appreciate his talents as a hunter and the determination he showed by bringing back everything he shot. Radisson's cunning had even almost gotten the better of them when he abandoned his geese and his musket. Then and there Ganaha was convinced of the young Frenchman's potential.

After travelling together for a few days, Ganaha was now certain that his prisoner would make a good hunter and an excellent warrior, as Iroquois custom demanded. Perhaps he would have his family adopt him to take the place of one of his fallen brothers. That would make his mother happy: she was hoping to adopt one or two French or Algonquin soldiers to make up for the many deaths that war and disease had brought to their family, their clan, and their village. Radisson's face was painted half red and half black, meaning that his fate remained in the balance: black for death, red for life. Ganaha was waiting until he knew his prisoner better before deciding one way or the other.

Radisson knew nothing of any of this. One night he had a surprising dream. He was back in Trois-Rivières with a Jesuit priest, eating roast goose and recounting his adventures while his sister Françoise served them beer. When he awakened, he took the dream to be a premonition and decided that he had a good chance of returning from his misadventure alive. From that day forth, he decided to forget about his friends François and Mathurin; in any case he could not bring them back. He decided to do everything he could to stay alive and to please his captors, especially Ganaha, his keeper. It didn't matter that the Iroquois had killed his friends. It didn't matter that it was his fault they were dead and he had been captured. Now, in the depths of his soul and conscience, nothing else must matter other than his life, and the survival he now believed to be possible.

From that moment on, Radisson pestered Ganaha every chance he got to teach him the Iroquois words that were soon to be a part of his vocabulary: canoe, sun, river, eat, drink, smile, friend, happiness... Whenever the group stopped to camp for the night, Radisson sang French songs to the great delight of his captors and joined in with their chants. He busied himself collecting firewood, he brought them water, and handed out food, doing everything he could to stay on their good side. Soon he realized that another Iroquois in his canoe, Ongienda, was Ganaha's brother. Knowing that now two of them trusted him, he tried to become friends with Ongienda. The strategy brought encouraging results: he was no longer bound, day or night. The fear that he might run away or take his revenge while they slept had disappeared. In the space of a few days, even though he could not understand why he was no longer being mistreated, Radisson was sincerely grateful to them. He even wondered if the French back in Trois-Rivières had not been exaggerating the cruelty of the Iroquois. And whenever he recalled the cold-blooded murder of François and Mathurin, he hastened to draw a black veil over their memory and devote all his thoughts, all his hopes, to the future.

Ten days after setting out up the river, the Iroquois landed at a place known for its good fishing. No sooner had they arrived than they each took up three-pronged harpoons and waited with them in the water at strategic spots. Radisson gestured to Ganaha that he wanted to fish and contribute to the meal. Knowing that the harpoon could be used as a dangerous weapon, his keeper hesitated. He glanced at Ongienda, who nodded his approval.

For the first time since his capture, Radisson held a weapon. He was happy and relieved to see that his captors trusted him. Eager to show himself worthy of their trust, he stood up to his waist in water on the sandy bottom at a gentle bend in the river, where, like the Iroquois around him, he waited patiently without moving. He held his harpoon tightly in his right hand, just above the water. Barely five minutes had gone by when an enormous fish came to a standstill right in front of him. Radisson couldn't believe his eyes. Gently moving its fins to stay just below the surface, the fish rested nonchalantly, indifferent to his presence.

What incredible good fortune! He was paralyzed for a moment, admiring the rainbow on the trout's back, lit up by the sun's rays shining through the clear river water. "God has given me this chance to win the Iroquois' esteem," he thought. Pulling himself together, he thrust the harpoon into his prey with all the force he could muster. The fish reacted so powerfully that it seemed as though it was going to explode! Radisson grabbed the harpoon tight and raced to the shoreline, just managing to keep the speared fish from wiggling off. The monster was struggling furiously. Radisson flung it down onto the sand and sank the harpoon deeper into its flesh with all his weight. The giant trout continued to flail about, this time with such strength that, once again, it almost escaped. But he kept the harpoon planted deep in the fish and the struggle quickly swung in his favour as sand flooded the gills of the deposed king of the river. It tired and suffocated. Soon, victory belonged to Radisson.

Extraordinarily proud of himself, he held up his trophy so that all his companions could see the enormous fish he had just caught. Radisson could feel tears welling in his eyes as he saw Ganaha run over, laughing and gesticulating wildly, showering him with words he didn't understand. His keeper took his harpoon from him for a moment and raised it high in the air before returning it to his protégé.

That evening all the Iroquois in the band were happy to share the giant trout, which they grilled over the fire with the other fish they'd caught. Radisson's was the biggest by far. He handed it out to his companions with indescribable joy, as though giving a precious gift to his family, and reserved the choicest cuts for Ganaha and Ongienda, who congratulated him. By the light of the fire, long after the sun had set, Ganaha painted Radisson's whole face red, talking to him non-stop, in high spirits. Radisson barely understood a word of it, but he felt the words flood over him as though he had always spoken Iroquois. He knew that his fate had taken a turn for the better. God was with him.

EVER SINCE the fishing episode, Radisson felt safe among his captors. They were visibly happy with him and increasingly treated him as one of their own. Radisson was at last getting the chance to travel and discover the world around him and began to forget some of his misfortune. For him, America was one surprise after another. He sometimes wondered if life as an Iroquois wasn't as worthwhile as life as a Frenchman.

They paddled across a beckoning lake. Radisson looked around in awe at the natural beauty all around him. He admired the greenery that cloaked the land in a host of dazzling shades. After a week of travelling south from Trois-Rivières to the region they were now passing through, the flora had been completely transformed. Uncertain new shoots had given way to lush foliage. Huge trees towered over the lake. In the distance, to the east and west, he saw mountains taller than any he had ever seen in France or New France. The canoes wove their way between peaceful wooded islets, as in a game of hide and seek. All around, the crystal-clear water abounded with fish and the forests teemed with game.

Once they reached the other side of the lake, they stopped for a long portage. The stronger members of the group carried the birch-bark canoes on their shoulders, while the others took the food, weapons, and ammunition. The trail was well marked and the Iroquois knew it by heart.

Ganaha showed more and more concern for Radisson, teaching him new words every day. Using gestures and a basic vocabulary that was growing by the day, they managed to communicate. Despite his delight, the young Frenchman couldn't help but wonder how a condemned man could so quickly become almost a brother. There was something he didn't understand about the Iroquois' attitude, something that made him suspicious. Something else might happen to turn them against him, he feared. Having completely lost his bearings, he had been overwhelmed by events and was in no position to think clearly.

After the portage, they put their canoes back into the river that flowed from the south and left the high mountains behind them. Tributaries swelled the river beneath them, driving them forward. In places, the water became so tumultuous that Radisson thought it would be better to get out and walk along the riverbank as they did before. But no. Despite the danger, the Iroquois plunged into the powerful rapids and tore down the river. Whenever the canoe began to toss about, Ganaha motioned for him to move to the back and keep still. Radisson contented himself with admiring his guides' strength and dexterity, even when the canoe took on water and the rocks came close to capsizing them. Ganaha and his brothers manoeuvred the canoe expertly and all ended up for the best.

After three days at this furious pace, the band stopped on an island that stretched almost all the way across the river. Another group of Iroquois had already set up camp there. They appeared to be from the same nation, but a different village. They greeted each other warmly and exchanged news. To everyone's surprise, a quarrel broke out between Ganaha and a young Iroquois from the other band who angrily remarked that Radisson hadn't even been roughed up. He was furious that a French prisoner was being treated so well. He wanted to see him suffer, to burn his flesh to show him who was in charge. Ganaha, who hoped to adopt Radisson and put him to good use working for his family, would hear nothing of doing him harm. Why torture a prisoner who had shown nothing but good will and had so many fine qualities? The young Iroquois from the other band shouted down each of these arguments and was determined to see the Frenchman punished like the enemy he was. Before the altercation could get out of control Ongienda intervened, warning the cocky young warrior their family affairs were no concern of his: "If you want our brother to suffer so much, go right ahead," he shouted. "Fight him yourself. If you win, he's all yours. Do whatever you like to him. But if you lose, he is ours and no one will so much as touch a hair on his head. Let's see who's stronger: you or him."

Radisson had been looking on from a distance. He realized they were talking about him because they pointed over at him more than once. What he didn't know yet was that Ongienda had challenged the young Iroquois to fight him. But he figured out what was going on soon enough when all the Iroquois formed a circle around him and his opponent, who was gearing up to fight. The youngster was taller but scrawnier than he was. They faced each other. Ongienda stood between them for a moment, apparently convinced that Radisson would come out on top, then stepped away and signalled for the fight to begin.

The young Iroquois threw himself at Radisson, punching and kicking him furiously. Radisson instantly understood that his life was in danger, so violent was the attack. His assailant's face was disfigured with cruelty. So Radisson fought back with the same rage. The fight was bitter. Blows rained down. Blood poured from their bodies. The Iroquois bit Radisson, who cried out in pain. Overcome by hatred and thanking God for having had him carry so many heavy barrels for his father, he threw his adversary to the ground. Radisson charged his rival and struck him with all his might. He pushed him, grabbed hold of him, knocked him to the ground. Mad with rage, the Iroquois countered with the energy born of despair. In a last-ditch effort, Radisson flung him to the ground again and, without giving him a second to fight back, dealt him a series of violent blows to the face, stomach, and head. The Iroquois was beaten. He curled up, broken and still. The fight was over.

Ganaha and Ongienda rushed over to Radisson proudly, shouting with joy. They held him tight in their arms and congratulated him on his strength and courage. Through the pain that was confounding his senses, their protégé realized that he had won. He was the stronger; he was saved. Thanks be to God! The Iroquois in his band showered their new recruit with praise and delighted in his exploit. They took him aside and stared at him in awe. In the meantime, the Iroquois in the other camp were resentful that a Frenchman had so clearly got the better of one of their own and tended to his wounds. It boded ill for them as they prepared to do battle along the St. Lawrence. They were furious, too, at the other members of their nation who had not only contributed to their humiliation but were now feting the man they refused to treat as a prisoner. The affront would have to be avenged.

For the rest of the day, tension between the two groups was palpable. On one side, Radisson was lavished with attention. Ongienda greased and combed his hair, someone else brought him food, and Ganaha again painted his whole face red. The other side held a meeting. Ganaha joined them in the evening and after much discussion it was agreed that, to maintain good relations between both groups and make up for the loss of the young warrior who was now injured and could no longer fight, two members of Ganaha's clan would accompany the Iroquois from the other village in their expedition against the French.

As Radisson licked his wounds, Ganaha and Ongienda sat around the fire with a man and a woman the Frenchman had never seen before. They talked long into the night, preparing to return to their village, making sure that something similar did not happen again.

WHEN HE AWAKENED, things seemed to have changed for Radisson. There was a strange feeling in the air. He couldn't see Ganaha anywhere. Ongienda curtly motioned for him to stand up and walk, then bound his hands behind his back as soon as he was distracted. Radisson didn't see it coming at all and had no time to react. As on his first day of captivity, a rope was tied around his neck. He was then shoved into a canoe. Radisson could not understand the sudden turn of events. He told himself he was right not to trust them and was annoyed that he'd dropped his guard. What was going to happen to him now? He feared the worst.

After a few minutes of paddling, an enormous waterfall blocked the way. They were forced to get out of the canoe and climb a steep path around the waterfall to continue their journey upriver. Radisson's whole body was aching from the fight. It was all he could to follow his captors up to the top of the headland without being able to use his hands. He felt humiliated and terribly vulnerable in spite of his resounding victory the night before.

Once they reached the top, as he clambered back into his canoe he noticed the woman Ganaha had been talking to the night before. She moved her canoe closer to his and spoke to him for a long time in a soft, comforting voice. In his confusion Radisson could not understand everything she said, only the words *brother*, *mother*, and *peace*. But her smile and the look in her eyes were comforting and full of compassion. She caressed Radisson's face and ran her fingers gently through his hair. How much better she made him feel! He would have given everything he had for her to stay close to him, by his side. But she was already moving away and motioned to Ongienda to leave. Propelled by four strong arms working extra hard against the slight current, the canoe advanced quickly and the kind woman dropped completely out of sight.

THEY SOON REACHED the Iroquois village. From the shore where he climbed out of the canoe, Radisson looked at the high stockade that no doubt hid dwellings behind it. A broad gate opened and dozens of people poured outside to form two long lines on either side. They were mostly women and children, but Radisson could also see a few teens and old men among them. They were all carrying sticks, whips, and bludgeons, shouting, crying, and stamping their feet with joy. Radisson felt as though he'd arrived at the gates of hell. He tried to back away, but Ongienda stopped him and shoved him forward.

Ganaha suddenly appeared amid the crowd. Radisson's hopes soared as soon as he saw him. Perhaps his keeper hadn't abandoned him after all. Then a woman well into middle age slid past Ganaha and strode purposefully in Radisson's direction. She was wearing an old leather dress and her long, dark hair hung down in braids on either side of a wrinkled face that still glowed with strength and energy. Short and bubbling with life, she pushed back the people lined up around her, gesticulating vigorously. She had no trouble elbowing aside a handful of boys who stood in her way. Ongienda stopped shoving Radisson and waited for the woman to reach them. He broke into a broad grin. Ganaha stood in the middle of the crowd and tried to disperse it. As soon as the woman reached Radisson, Ongienda and his companions hurried to lend Ganaha a hand. In a firm voice she told Radisson: "I am Ganaha's and Ongienda's mother and you are my son. You owe me obedience. Now follow me."

She took him by the arm and led him to the village. They caught up with Ganaha after a few steps and the other warriors immediately formed a circle around them. Despite furious protests from a few angry Iroquois, the twelve men forced their way through the crowd and into the village. Radisson's new mother didn't seem to hear the protests. Straight ahead she ploughed, still leading her new son by the arm.

Once past the stockade, the group made a beeline for a long building made from bark. They moved inside, posting two warriors by the gate so that no undesirables could follow them in. Intimidated at first, Radisson didn't dare move in the half-light. The others motioned for him to move to the middle of the longhouse, where Ganaha quickly untied him. Gesturing and with the help of simple words, pronounced slowly, he did his best to explain to Radisson that he was now safe with his brothers, his mother Katari, and the other members of his clan, the Bear clan.

Even though Radisson understood most of Ganaha's reassurances, even though his keeper appeared to have once more become as friendly as he had been on their best days together on the canoe trip, he still could not quite believe his new-found freedom. His confidence had been shaken. Recent events had made him wary. Radisson was almost certain to have avoided being ill-treated by the other Iroquois in the village. But for how much longer? And why were all those people so intent on beating him? He hoped he would be safe in his new home but, after everything he had been through over the past few weeks, he still had misgivings. His companions' good humour soon put him at ease, though. Concluding that the best policy would be to look happy, he embraced Ganaha and gave his new mother a kiss.

A NEW FAMILY?

THE VILLAGE was almost deserted: all the men had gone off to war. The longhouse of the Bear clan, which Radisson was now part of, was almost empty, even though it could hold at least one hundred. Katari had never seen so many absent at the same time. Only the women, children, and those too old to fight were left behind. And she was not happy. With everyone gone, the women had to do all the work. Radisson was sad there were only young boys to keep him company. He was forced to spend most of his time with Katari's two daughters, who were almost his age. The prettier of the two, Conharassan, showered him with affection, always looking for a chance to caress and kiss him, egged on by her mother. Radisson didn't know how to react. His mother—his real mother back in France, his mother who went to mass every day and was so afraid of sin—would never have allowed a brother and sister to have such a relationship. Radisson was finding it hard to adapt to so many differences all at once. To put his mind at ease, he spent as much time as he could with Katari.

He followed her out to the fields and did whatever she asked of him. He hoed and turned over the soil while she told him tales of the French Jesuit who had spent a few weeks in her village, several years ago. He told them that Frenchmen worked the fields, that they were proud of their work and that the Iroquois should do the same. Katari agreed with him. But Radisson could see that only people from other nations—prisoners—helped the women tend the crops of corn, beans, and squash. He quickly learned from the jibes aimed at him by the youngsters in the village that it was no work for a free man, or a warrior. But Radisson could also see that he was not a prisoner like the others. He stopped fending off Conharassan's advances and made love to her whenever he liked. He was even beginning to appreciate the affection she lavished on him every day. He was also free to come and go as he pleased. He could go hunting just outside the village with the other boys. But those who were kept prisoner were nothing more than slaves, at the beck and call of the village women who ordered them around.

Despite his freedom, he didn't go hunting very often. His young companions were all too keen to laugh at him. He was French, after all, a captured enemy ... and he did women's work. He found his life here rather monotonous, truth be told. He had no friends. Conharassan was nice to him, of course, but he had to be careful, to keep his most intimate thoughts and feelings to himself. His best friend was a dog, a big, brown, friendly, clever-looking dog that took to following him around shortly after he arrived. Radisson started feeding it, petting it, and the two quickly became firm friends. He called him Bo, this dog who became his confidant. Whenever the two of them were alone, he spoke to him in French: "You know how I miss them, don't you, boy? You understand, don't you? I miss them all, Marguerite, François, Françoise..." Each time he felt a pang of anguish. He preferred not to dwell on the tragic event that had changed his life forever and brought an end to the lives of his two friends. Would he be able to return to Trois-Rivières and see his family again one day, he wondered. "Can you help me find the way back, boy? Think I can make it? Tell me, Bo. Tell me." Whenever he talked to his dog like that, Radisson felt guilty for living with the people who had killed his French friends.

GANAHA WAS BACK! Radisson was overjoyed. He hadn't realized how attached he had become to his abductor. Katari hadn't told him that Ganaha had gone to fetch their father, but now he was back with Garagonké, who now became Radisson's adoptive father. Garagonké appeared just as suddenly in Radisson's life as his real father back in France had left it, without a trace. Ganaha had taken three weeks to find him and bring him home. Garagonké had been travelling from one Cayuga and Seneca village to the next, planning the next offensive. Ganaha had spoken so highly of his new son that Garagonké agreed to interrupt his mission.

Radisson was very impressed by the war chief who had put together strings of victories and killed so many enemies. Despite his venerable age, the energy and dignity he emanated reminded Radisson of the traits he so admired in the Algonquin chief at Trois-Rivières. In silence, Garagonké looked his new son over from head to toe for long seconds before addressing him. Radisson felt the invincible warrior's stare pierce right through him.

"Ganaha did not lie to me," he said. "You are indeed my son, the incarnation of Orinha whom you are replacing. Welcome to our family. The Bear clan welcomes you with joy into its longhouse. Speak to me, now. Your father wishes to hear your voice."

Troubled by shameful thoughts, Radisson could not think of a single word. What should he say to a war chief from a nation that had killed so many French? Through what metamorphosis could he have become such a welcoming father? Radisson opted to speak to him of hunting and fishing, knowing that an Iroquois must be good at both. He hoped Garagonké would be pleased with him.

"Fine," his father replied. "You must hunt more often. A man's place is not in the longhouse with the women. Ganaha praised your strength and I see he spoke the truth. You fought an Iroquois who wanted you dead and you beat him. Good. If you fight our enemies with the same conviction, you will bring honour to our family and to our nation. That is what I expect from you. But you are still young and have much to learn. Your two brothers and your uncles will guide you once they return from their campaigns. As for me, I must complete my missions to the other Iroquois nations. We will have time enough to get to know each other this winter."

The power of his voice, his assurance, and his presence impressed Radisson, who felt even more intimidated. He was not at all certain he was the warrior his father hoped for. He was not even certain he would be able to become a true Iroquois. And yet he knew his life depended on his ability to transform himself. He had to. It was the only path to salvation open to him.

The same evening, Garagonké told Radisson about his father, his grandfather, and his great-grandfather, all valiant warriors from the Wolf and the Tortoise clans. He paid tribute to the woman he had married, Katari, and to the other women in the Bear clan, whose many children contributed to the village's well-being, each in their own way. Once he had finished, in front of all those seated in a circle at the centre of the longhouse, around a fire now reduced to embers, Garagonké moved his hands with a broad, sweeping motion and said to his son: "All this is yours. Now you know the history of your family. Tell me, are you happy to be living among us?" Radisson could only nod his approval. Then, after a moment's hesitation, he replied with conviction: "Yes!" How much better he felt now that he'd met his father.

That night, above Ganaha's bed, Radisson slept soundly on a bed of fir boughs, wrapped in a soft, pliable deerskin. Opposite him, on the other side of the family fire, Katari slept on the bed closest to the ground, her husband in the bed above her. Beside them, Radisson's two sisters slept in bunk beds. But Ongienda's bed lay empty. He had returned to war.

RADISSON'S FATHER and brother left the next day: Ganaha, to the neighbouring Oneida nation to join a war party and Garagonké on his mission to the chiefs of the Iroquois nations to the west in hopes of launching a great offensive the following summer. Radisson once again found himself alone.

A few days later, while Radisson was working in the fields with his two sisters, a rumour began to make the rounds among the women. In no time at all, they were feverish with excitement. Conharassan and Assasné, Radisson's other sister, dashed back to the village without even waiting for him, and many of the other women followed them as fast as they could. Surprised at the commotion, Radisson followed them slowly, observing closely in an attempt to understand what was causing the excitement. As he got closer to the village gate, he could make out a group of armed Iroquois dressed for war in the distance. At the same time, women, boys, and a handful of old men rushed to take up positions outside the stockade, row upon row, on each side of the gate. Once again, each brandished a stick, an iron bar, a pestle for grinding corn, a whip, or a thorny branch. Others still hurried to take their places, jostling for position.

It resembled the scene that greeted Radisson when he first arrived in the village as a prisoner a few weeks before. Curious to see what would happen next, he joined the throng by the gate, ready to slip away if the crowd turned against him. Experience had taught him he could never be too careful with the Iroquois. As soon as she saw him, his sister Conharassan leaped into his arms, beside herself with excitement. She was holding a long switch in one hand and a branch covered with thorns in the other. She thrust the switch into his hand, keeping the more threatening branch for herself.

Nearly everyone who lived in the village was now lined up in one of two long rows on either side of the gate. Assasné ran to take her place with two friends. They quickly positioned themselves at the end of the row. Only Katari was missing. Radisson could not see her anywhere.

The clamour of the crowd welcomed the warriors back to the village after a successful raid. Behind them they dragged three prisoners, held together by a rope around their necks. They were all braves from enemy nations. As they drew closer, the cries grew louder. After a brief hesitation, a first prisoner threw himself between the two lines of villagers, who lashed out at him with all their might. Radisson admired the courage and agility of the man, who covered his head with his arms and managed to dodge an assailant or two. He progressed quickly, not letting the beating slow him down. Conharassan, both arms in the air, was jubilant and struck him on the way past as hard as she could. Ripping open his back with her thorn-covered branch, she shrieked with excitement. Radisson watched the poor prisoner pass by, not moving a muscle. He saw his swollen face and his eyes aglow with terror. Blood ran down from his scalp, off his back and legs. With one final effort, the man flung himself to the ground just inside the stockade, exhausted. Nobody would beat him now. Radisson would have liked to help him, but that would have been too risky. He would probably be attacked as well. He restrained himself.

The roar of the crowd welled up again, signalling that the second prisoner was on his way. As with the first, the women and boys struck him with determined, vicious blows. The man stumbled and picked himself up again. Three people broke ranks to beat him with a stick. The prisoner swayed, zigzagged, and ran into other attackers. His head and body were lacerated and bleeding profusely. Radisson could hardly breathe at the sight of the senseless spectacle. He felt every blow as though it were aimed at him. The man fell a second time, just in front of Conharassan, who restrained herself and did not hit him, perhaps out of pity. More dead than alive, the man crawled on all fours to the village, a woman continuing to whip him all the while. With great difficulty, he managed to cross the boundary line that spared him a further beating.

Conharassan let out a shrill cry and dashed toward the third prisoner, who, rooted to the spot in terror, refused to advance. His captors shoved him forward. A group broke off from the crowd to beat him. Women and boys battered him senseless. He stood no chance. Wielding her thorn-covered branch, Conharassan joined the pack that was determined to finish him off then and there. Radisson could not bear to watch the savage execution and slipped away when nobody was watching. He ran between the longhouses until he reached the home of the Bear clan, which he entered at full speed.

Once he got his breath back, he saw Katari sitting pensively beside the fire. When Radisson walked over to her, she stood up, opened her arms, and held him tightly against her chest, murmuring in his ear: "My dear son... I am so glad nothing happened to you. I was worried." Radisson felt a surge of affection for his adoptive mother, the mother who had taken no part in the torture, the mother who had protected him from the same horrible ordeal when he had arrived in the village. If it weren't for her and Ganaha, he realized, he might well be dead. They would have smashed his head in, ripped off his skin, and slashed open his stomach. He did not know how he would have reacted under such a deluge of blows.

Katari told him a story he could only half understand, but he caught enough to guess at the reasons why she didn't attend the beating. Outside, Radisson could hear the commotion of the crowd that had come back inside the village. The Iroquois were preparing a torture session for the two prisoners who had survived.

"I saw my parents die before my eyes," said Katari, "when I was six years old. The Iroquois tortured them. They had captured us Hurons—their enemies—in an ambush. Because I was a child they spared me. A family from the Bear clan adopted me. Later, I became an Iroquois, a good-looking, hard-working woman who knew how to love. Garagonké fell in love with me and married me. And I loved him too."

Radisson was struck by the emotion he could hear in his mother's pained voice.

"I never did get used to the torture. I don't want to add to the hatred and the thirst for vengeance that too many of us feel. Killing is no way to strike a balance between the living and the dead, no matter what they say. There is no end to the cycle of vengeance. Death is everywhere now, spread by war and disease. The spirits have abandoned the Iroquois. I adopted you to replace my son who was killed in battle. I asked Ganaha to bring me back a prisoner because that's how tradition would have it, the real tradition that adds a new life for each that is taken away. Adopting new blood makes our family grow and strengthens our hold on life. That's what will save us."

Katari broke off for a long moment. She looked Radisson straight in the eye, holding his face in her hands. She smiled at him and asked: "Do you know why the spirits are no longer protecting the Iroquois? Do you think they're angry with us? Do you think it is their turn for revenge?"

Radisson did not completely understand the question, but he was sure he did not know the answer. The subject was far beyond what he knew of life and the Iroquois language. He chose to say nothing. Katari looked away and lowered her arms.

"The Great Spirit of the French is powerful," she continued, staring off into space. "I saw it when the Blackrobe your father captured six years ago spent a few months here living under our roof. He learned Iroquois and would often speak to us of peace, of peace and love. Even though he was our prisoner, he was very powerful. The spirit he worshipped gave him the strength to live and to convince us we were better off selling him to the Dutch rather than killing him. Perhaps he was right about everything."

Katari looked at Radisson again, with eyes so full of compassion, so sad, and so mysterious that he lost himself in them.

"Garagonké still believes in war," she continued. "He believes that waging ruthless war against all the enemies of the Iroquois will save our people. May he be right. May the spirits that have always supported him stay favourable to him and bring us victory. But doubt has started to flicker in my mind. I am afraid for him and I am afraid for my people because we are dying in greater numbers than the French and the Dutch. Their Great Spirit is more powerful than the spirits of our ancestors."

Katari fell silent. Radisson too kept silent, more touched than if he had understood everything. His mother was calling him to her rescue, he thought, but he did not know how to answer her call. Would he ever be able to? He had his doubts. She had saved his life and yet he felt as though there was nothing he could do for her. It was a sad situation, but one day he hoped he could turn around and pay back the debt he owed her.

Also lost in her thoughts, Katari poked distractedly at the fire with the end of a long stick. Radisson asked her why she didn't try to save the prisoners as she had done for him. She threw back her head and gave him a piercing look. "Because the prisoners were brought back by the Tortoise clan and I am from the Bear clan. There is nothing I can do for them. Listen to them…" Radisson could hear them screaming in the distance. "They have already started to torture them. Tomorrow, they will kill them. But it will be a long, drawn-out affair—they know how to make them suffer. Until then, you will stay here with me. It's not a good idea for them to see a Frenchman. Who knows what might happen to you? The warriors do not know you and might turn on you. Stay here. With me, you have nothing to fear."

ONCE CALM HAD RETURNED to the village, Radisson took his father's advice and organized a short hunting expedition. Serontatié, the only boy he liked spending time with, would accompany him. Despite his youth, he was kind, smart, and quick-witted. And, above all else, he never treated Radisson with contempt, always as an equal. Still, as a token of his friendship toward Serontatié, Radisson had to agree that two of his friends from the Wolf clan would join them. Even though he had no affinity toward the other two, he was in no position to complain. His dog Bo would accompany the party.

While Serontatié and Radisson both opted for a musket, their companions felt more comfortable with bow and arrow. Each one brought with him a knife, a tomahawk, and a fire starter. As a precaution they carried a small reserve of cornmeal.

At the start of their journey, the four young men wandered through the forest without encountering any sign of big game. They amused themselves killing hares and squirrels along the way. Through his innate sense of pride and because he felt he had to prove his worth to Serontatié's two friends who were enjoying making fun of him, Radisson tried his best to impress them with his shooting prowess. Ever since he saw the prisoners tortured then put to death, he had felt an even greater need to show off his strength and skills. But to show their superiority the two fools accompanying them fell back on their bows and arrows, weapons they mastered much better than Radisson. Radisson suffered their jibes in silence, but he could hardly wait to shut them up the first chance he could get. Wisely, he managed to keep everyone focused on hunting, the passion they all shared.

As the four companions were looking for a good spot to set up camp, they met an old man out hunting alone in the woods. He introduced himself as an Algonquin by birth, adopted by the Iroquois in a neighbouring village four years ago. He enjoyed his new life. His only regret was not becoming an Iroquois earlier, he said. And he was not shy about his talents as a hunter and warrior. Impressed, the four young men held a quick confab to decide if they should press on with this experienced hunter. Later that evening, they would share a stew with him, made from two of the hares he had killed along with their own. And then in the days to come, they would be able to rely on his experience to flush out bigger game. The arrangement suited them and they quickly agreed to continue with the Algonquin.

As the hares were roasting over the fire, the man could not stop talking. He went on at length about his hunting exploits, complaining that there wasn't much game around the Iroquois villages compared to where he came from, north of the St.

Lawrence. He knew a great place to hunt, he told them, east of where they were, and offered to take them there the next day. There, he told them, they'd be close to the Dutch colony, where almost nobody hunted, and where they'd be sure to bag themselves some big game. The young men agreed.

A little later, having noticed that he looked different, the Algonquin questioned Radisson about his origins.

"You're not an Iroquois, are you?"

"I'm French," replied Radisson. "I was adopted two months ago by a family from the Bear clan. I live in the village of Coutu, not far from here. I am happy there."

Since the situation was clear enough for all to see, Radisson's companions felt a little uncomfortable, but preferred not to let their feelings show.

"I've met a Frenchman or two in my time," the former Algonquin continued. "If you ask me, you'll be far better off with the Iroquois. They're the best warriors in the world. Great hunters, too—although not as good as the Algonquins."

Enthralled by the incessant chatter of their new acquaintance, the three young Iroquois let him take over the conversation completely. Radisson found it all somewhat strange.

"That your dog?" he asked.

Radisson nodded. "Come here, boy. Here's something to eat." The Algonquin threw Bo a scrap of meat, which he swallowed with a single gulp. "You know that a hunting dog can come in very useful?" he continued. "I'll show you tomorrow. Unless you've been bad to him, he'll help us track our game. You'll soon see I know what I'm doing. Like hunting, do you?"

"Yes," Radisson replied.

"Like travelling, do you?" the mysterious Algonquin asked him again. "The best hunting grounds are far from here, you know. We could all head west together, head for the mountains."

No one replied.

"I'll lead the way," added the Algonquin. "You'll see, Radisson. Have some more, boy."

And the Algonquin threw Bo another chunk of meat. His interest in the dog was beginning to get on Radisson's nerves. Like he was trying to win it over. It was his dog, after all, his faithful companion, not some stranger's. Anyways, there was no way he'd be telling him its name.

"When I was back home," the man went on, "every winter we would go hunting with our dogs, great big dogs, much bigger than this one here. And we would always return home with more game than our toboggans could carry."

At nightfall, after turning the young men's heads with his fine words, the Algonquin stepped away from the fire for a moment. A bit later, he motioned to Radisson to join him: he wanted to show him tracks he said had been left by game. But no matter how closely they stared, Radisson couldn't see a thing. Bo didn't either, although that didn't stop him from sniffing all around them excitedly. As soon as they had their backs turned and the three Iroquois couldn't hear them, the man asked Radisson under his breath if he spoke Algonquin.

"A little," he replied.

Delighted, the man continued in his mother tongue.

"Want to go back to Trois-Rivières?" he asked. "I know the way. It'll be easy if there are two of us. What do you say?"

Taken aback by a proposal that came completely out of the blue, in a language that reminded him terribly of Trois-Rivières, Radisson was speechless.

"Do you understand me?" the man continued, repeating his question and this time motioning with his hands. "You," he pointed to Radisson. "Go back to Trois-Rivières with me." He touched his chest. "Trois-Rivières." He held up three fingers. "You and me together." He wrapped one finger around the other. "What do you say?"

Radisson nodded to show he understood the question. But the Algonquin's eyes lit up immediately. In his mind Radisson had just said yes.

"Here's my plan," the Algonquin went on. "We'll bump off your three companions in their sleep, then make a run for my canoe, which is hidden close by. What do you say?"

Radisson shook his head violently, but the Algonquin wasn't taking no for an answer.

"The Iroquois hate the French! Sooner or later they'll kill you! I'm your only way out! Do what I say and everything will be fine! Let's go. Your friends will be getting suspicious."

Radisson was rattled. He tried to convince himself that he had misunderstood. But he knew enough Algonquin to understand that this man wanted to kill his companions and run off with him to Trois-Rivières. TROIS-RIVIÈRES! His head seemed to explode at the very thought of it. His sisters, his friends, his language, and the stockade he should never have left. He was giddy at the very prospect. But he didn't want to kill his companions, especially not Serontatié, his friend. What was he to do? His stomach was tying itself in knots. His belly was so sore he had to bend over. And yet he couldn't give anything away in case his companions suspected they might be in danger. If they did, they would kill him.

Radisson was in over his head. How he would have loved to talk it over with the Algonquin and find some other way. Wait until the next day at least. Come up with another plan. But they dared not mention anything in front of the three Iroquois. Radisson did not know what to do. If he wandered off with the man again on his own, his companions would definitely know something was up. He felt trapped; a downcast look came over his face. Afraid that his plan would be found out, the Algonquin started to worry and began talking non-stop to the three Iroquois to create a diversion. He asked them about their favourite weapons, when they started hunting, about their families, their village. The discussion was going fine until the Algonquin turned to Radisson and asked him in Algonquin when he learned to hunt. Téganissorens jumped angrily to his feet.

"What did you ask him?" he shouted.

"I asked him when he learned to hunt," the Algonquin replied calmly, this time in Iroquois.

"And why are you talking to him in your language?"

"He speaks Algonquin and I wanted to talk to him in my own language, that's all," the Algonquin said nonchalantly.

"You're an Iroquois now! So speak Iroquois like the rest of us! Got it?"

Now that he was sure the three youngsters could not understand him, he said one last thing to Radisson in his mother tongue, as blandly as possible.

"Quit moping around like that! They'll think we're up to something. Make an effort. Smile."

"Stop it!" Téganissorens snapped. "You're both Iroquois and you will speak Iroquois! Otherwise you will be treated as enemies! I'm not going to say it a third time!"

"Fine, fine," the Algonquin replied. "I was just telling him we'll have to stop speaking Algonquin to each other. It's over. Calm down."

The matter was settled. The five men let the fire die down and sleep began to get the better of Radisson's companions, who didn't suspect a thing. Before turning in, the Algonquin found a way to encourage his accomplice, who still looked distraught.

"Get plenty of rest," he told Radisson in Iroquois. "Tomorrow we'll head east, out to where the Dutch are. It's a long way, but it'll be worth it. I'll take you to the best hunting ground in the whole world. You'll be happy and your friends will have all the time they need to rest. Don't worry."

But panic swept over Radisson. On the one hand, he dreamed of seeing Marguerite and his friends in Trois-Rivières again, of eating the French bread he had always eaten in Trois-Rivières and Paris. He could already smell the pots simmering over the hearth, could hear everyone chattering away—in French—around the table. On the other hand, the price to be paid was exorbitant: he would have to kill Serontatié, who had never done him any harm, as well as his two companions. It was a dreadful situation. How was he possibly going to get out of it?

Everyone was asleep except Radisson. He couldn't very well expose the Algonquin: he had such a way with words. In two seconds flat, he'd have convinced Téganissorens that *Radisson* was plotting to kill his Iroquois brothers and run away. Denouncing him would bring certain death. He cursed the Algonquin for pushing him so hard. Radisson would have much preferred to wait for the right moment, the next day or perhaps the day after next. He would have liked to wake the Algonquin up to talk things over and change their plan, but he stayed where he was since his Iroquois companions weren't yet sleeping soundly. He would have to bide his time. He reassured himself, stroking Bo, who was dozing now by his side. Only the moon and the stars cast their feeble light over the forest. Radisson finally fell into a deep sleep.

A hand touched Radisson on the shoulder and he awoke with a start. The Algonquin motioned to him to get to his feet, handing him a tomahawk. He pointed to Serontatié's prostrate body, motioning for him to kill him. Radisson didn't even have time to protest: the Algonquin had already smashed his tomahawk over Otreouti's head from point-blank range. His brain exploded over their legs. Bo began to howl. The two other Iroquois jumped to their feet to defend themselves and the Algonquin struck Téganissorens' head with the butt of his musket. The young man collapsed in a heap. But Radisson was paralyzed. He couldn't kill his friend. Serontatié rushed at him, knife in hand, and only just missed him as Radisson's reflexes kicked in at the very last second and he ducked to avoid the fatal blow. He wheeled around and planted his tomahawk in Serontatié's skull. The Iroquois gave out a long groan, wobbled, and fell to the ground. The Algonquin picked up his bag, shouting at Radisson to hurry. Bo was barking and growling fiercely.

Radisson tried to do as he ordered, but his tomahawk was stuck in his friend's skull. He didn't want to leave it there. It was too horrible, too cruel. He had to pull it out. But, try as he might, it wouldn't budge. Radisson planted his foot on Serontatié's bloody face and pulled with all his strength! At last it gave way, and Radisson almost fell backward with the effort. Completely overcome by the turn events had taken, he slid his blood-covered tomahawk into his belt and caught up with his accomplice. He quickly gathered up his bag and musket, and called his dog. But the Algonquin wouldn't hear of bringing him along. "Filthy beast!" he shouted, flinging a stone in its direction. Radisson called him again. "Here, Bo! Come with me, boy!" But the Algonquin slapped him across the face: "Are you nuts?" he cried. "Your dog's staying put! If we take it with us, the Iroquois will hear the barking from miles around. They'll catch up with us in no time. You really want to die? Now follow me and do what I tell you!" Radisson was broken-hearted. But now that his life was in the hands of this stranger, there was nothing for it but to do as he said.

At first light, they reached the spot where the Algonquin's canoe lay hidden. They threw it into the water and started paddling as fast as they could. In the pale light of the new day, Bo followed them from afar, barking at them from the shore, as if to say, "Take me with you, Radisson!" Distraught, the young Frenchman looked back for an instant and watched his dear companion disappear forever.

RADISSON WAS CONVINCED the Iroquois were hot on their heels and would slaughter them at any moment. He paddled with the energy born of desperation. They needed to get as far away as they could, as quickly as they could. The Algonquin didn't even want to stop when night came. At first light the next day, after twenty-four hours of uninterrupted exertion, they finally set foot on dry land. After carefully hiding the canoe, they took refuge in the woods to rest for the day. The stop gave Radisson time to think over everything that had just happened to him: another tragic event.

The Algonquin, who was called Negamabat, laid out the rules for the entire journey: they would travel only at night and rest during the day, when they would hide from the Iroquois in the woods. They must not talk during the day, but could whisper to each other, only when strictly necessary, at night.

Radisson felt betrayed. He now understood that Negamabat used him to make his getaway, used his youthful strength and endurance, because alone Negamabat could never have managed to paddle so far, so quickly, through so much danger. He had guessed that Radisson shared his desire to return to Trois-Rivières to be reunited with his family and had taken full advantage of it. Radisson was haunted by the murder of Serontatié. How bitterly he regretted it. Bringing about the death of his three companions had only put his own life in jeopardy. Now Katari, Ganaha, and Garagonké would hate him and all the Iroquois would search for him everywhere, their hearts filled with rage. If they found him, they would slaughter him without pity. What a mess!

Radisson hated Negamabat for dragging him into this terrible situation. He hated him even more when he realized he hadn't even bothered to take their victims' bows and arrows so they could hunt without making a sound. There was no way they could use muskets: that would draw too much attention to themselves. Fishing in the river was also too risky. With so little to eat, Radisson's stomach was beginning to grumble. Berries and roots were not enough. The journey back to Trois-Rivières was shaping up to be arduous indeed.

For three nights, they paddled back down the river that Radisson had gone up as a prisoner. The Algonquin knew the way like the back of his hand; at least he had been telling the truth. Their days of half-sleep and worry were no better than half-restful. The task facing them was huge. Gradually, Radisson's cold fury gave way to a cold analysis of the situation. Now that he had made the fatal mistake of killing the very people who had welcomed him as a son, there was no going back. All he could hope for was to make good his escape. They must reach New France and find refuge there at all costs. He poured all his energy and intelligence into reaching their goal. Even though he hated Negamabat, he had to acknowledge his cool-headedness and his skill, his courage and his stamina. Whether they were navigating along the water in the dark, dragging their canoe up onto the bank to avoid rapids, or forced to portage, Negamabat remained a dependable guide. In this regard, Radisson trusted him completely.

All the same, the long days of waiting were unbearable.

For three days in a row, Radisson broke one of the Algonquin's rules. He armed himself with a long stick and went hunting, not far away from their hideaway. And it was just as well he did: for two days running, he managed to kill a porcupine. The raw meat they wolfed down restored some of their energy. On the third day, he returned empty-handed, and on the fourth day of his dissent, as Radisson was getting ready to venture out despite the furious looks from Negamabat, he saw three Iroquois canoes coming toward them. From the ridge where they had set up their camp, well back from the shore, they could see that the Iroquois were wearing war paint. They were paddling slowly, looking around them intently. One of their canoes moved toward the shore, another skirted past an islet. They were on the lookout... on the lookout *for them*, no doubt. A feeling of terror washed over Radisson. Even though their canoe was well hidden, it would not have taken much for them to be discovered and massacred. From that moment on, he gave up hunting during the day and stayed hidden instead. Not moving a muscle.

The following night, beneath a pale quarter moon, the two fugitives carefully made their way across a large, dark lake to flee as far away as possible. Along the way they could make out the flames of an Iroquois campfire in the distance and hear disjointed chanting. It sounded angry, threatening.

As the days passed, Radisson felt his strength abandoning him. In his exhaustion he replayed the fatal blow he dealt Serontatié over and over in his mind, and saw the moment when he tried to dislodge the tomahawk from his friend's skull. In his nightmare, he could never manage to do it. It stayed there forever, as though the irreparable could never be forgotten. The murder haunted Radisson like no other event in his life. Cold, heavy, uninterrupted rain only added to his distress. The two were terribly cold. But they dared not light a fire, lest the Iroquois spot it. Their powder was damp, useless. Now they were weaponless and more vulnerable than ever.

Radisson and Negamabat spent a hellish night hurtling through rapids they could not see in the dark. At every moment, their lives were in danger. But perhaps there was a god for fugitives, for they made it through the night unscathed.

The next day, after they had recovered a little, Radisson gnawed at a few bitter roots before spending the rest of the day stretched out on his back. He was careful not to get too close to Negamabat, whom he both cursed and thanked God for, depending on the hour of the day. His eyes turned heavenward, he saw his whole life flash before him, as though in a dream. He thought about his father, his real father back in France, who disappeared without a word of explanation and was never seen again. Perhaps he was kidnapped, or murdered, or killed in an accident. Radisson was now more aware of these possibilities, whereas before he had always believed his father had abandoned him, his mother, and his younger sister. Life could be so unpredictable, so fragile. But whether his father disappeared of his own volition or not did not change the pain he felt. His thoughts that day could not heal the wound. Then and there, Radisson swore that if he ever reached Trois-Rivières alive, never again would he let anyone dictate his life. Never again would a Negamabat push him around or tell him what to do. He would seize his life by the scruff of the neck and make it his own, as if breaking in a horse.

Radisson and the Algonquin at last reached the St. Lawrence. By this time, the lights and shadows of the night were playing tricks on Radisson. He was completely exhausted, mentally and physically. But he found hope. A few more hours paddling and he would be saved. Unfortunately, day dawned on them still far from Trois-Rivières. They would have to resign themselves once more to hiding for a whole day. They waded through the long grass of Lake Saint-Pierre to hide their canoe. They made it to the muddy bank—back where it all began— when despair engulfed Radisson.

After a long pause, Negamabat broke their self-imposed rules and told Radisson to wait for him there while he went on to Trois-Rivières.

"I'm taking the canoe. You wait for me here. As soon as I've returned to my Algonquin brothers, we'll let the French know and they'll come and get you. If no one comes within a day that means I'm dead. You'll have to return to Trois-Rivières on foot, along the shore. Farewell."

"No! Don't go!" pleaded Radisson. "We have to stick together. Wait for nightfall. Wait for me…"

But the Algonquin disappeared into the long grass. He did not look back or answer Radisson.

"Wait!" Radisson shouted again. "Wait!"

"Good luck!" Negamabat grunted to him from afar.

Radisson's whole body was shaking. He could not bear the thought of dying here, of hunger or cold. For the first time, he thought of how Pierre Godefroy, François' father, would react when he heard the news of his return. "Radisson!" he would cry. "The scoundrel who led my son to his death? Let him starve! That's all he deserves." Abandoned, once again.

Without a second thought, Radisson caught up with Negamabat, just in time to leap into the canoe with him. "Too bad," he thought. "I'll live or die with the man who got me into this."

Their canoe slid out of the long grass and headed toward Trois-Rivières. The sun warmed their bodies and re-energized them. At last, the river began to narrow. They were getting closer. Ahead of them, an object appeared in midstream. Negamabat stood up, and put his hand to his forehead to get a better look. It looked like a heron. He sat back down and said, "Let's go," picking up his paddle. Radisson trusted his judgment and began paddling again as best he could. But as they drew closer to the object, which was getting bigger by the minute, it didn't take long for them to realize their mistake. It was not a heron at all, but a canoe full of Iroquois bearing down on them, eight warriors giving it their all, propelling their canoe forward at frightening speed. Their only chance of escaping with their lives was to head straight for shore and hide in the forest. They needed to be quick, but they were both bone tired...

The tips of the first bulrushes thrusting out of the water slowed their canoe. Dry land was too far away for them to jump ashore. They would have to keep paddling. But the Iroquois were gaining on them with every stroke. Three shots rang out. Negamabat was hit and fell face down into the canoe, bleeding heavily. Radisson thought of jumping into the water to avoid the next round of fire. But it was too deep to walk in and the long grass was too thick for him to swim. The enemy canoe drew alongside him and four powerful arms grabbed hold of him. The Iroquois hauled him aboard and beat him, then tied a rope around his neck and bound his hands. One of them pulled out a fingernail with his teeth. Pain shot through his body, but Radisson did not even have the strength to scream. He let go of reality, as everything around him collapsed.

CHAPTER 4

TORTURE

T HE IROQUOIS MANHANDLED Radisson all the way back to the village. Famished, disheartened, he endured it all without complaint, without resisting. He thought only of saving his energy and his life, if such a thing were still possible.

As they crossed the broad lake that separated the north-flowing from the south-flowing waters, they encountered a group of Iroquois from the village where Radisson lived. After negotiation, the five warriors from the Wolf clan, who had been looking everywhere for Radisson for the past three weeks, roared with joy when they finally got their hands on him in return for a wampum, a necklace made from shells. Even though the Iroquois looked after him and did not ill-treat him, Radisson was under no illusions: his fate was sealed. He knew well that the stronger the prisoner, the better it reflected on the warriors who captured him. His captors would want to put on a good show when they hauled him back to the village like a trophy, before they killed him.

Even so, Radisson devoured everything he was allowed to eat. He wanted to regain his strength so he could fight to the finish, even if he had only one chance in one hundred thousand of coming out alive. A single thought filled his mind: he must LIVE at all costs! No matter his past mistakes, his past glories, his family, his pain, his dreams, he would do everything he could to cheat death. And if the end did come, then he wanted to leave this world head held high: bravely, not as a traitor or a coward.

When they got to within sight of the village, Radisson's guard suddenly yanked the rope around his neck. Despite the shock, he used all his determination and agility to stay on his feet. The five Iroquois who bought him joined some thirty triumphant warriors who were openly roughing up the dozen or so men and women they had captured. It was a triumph for the village. People were running in all directions, shouting with joy. Even if the fear of dying was gnawing at him, Radisson clenched his teeth and stood as straight as an oak to maintain his dignity and show his courage. His dark eyes gleamed with an unquenchable thirst for life. He knew he had only one chance if he was to avoid death: he must prove his outstanding courage and valour to all. It was his last card, and he intended to play it with a flourish.

Many of the village men had returned home from their war parties. They gathered in rows on either side of the village gate alongside the women and children, primed to take part in the sinister welcoming ceremony. All were armed. The welcome promised to be even more terrible than the one Radisson had witnessed a few weeks before. The guards still had their prisoners on leashes like animals and were preparing to set them loose into the madness. Radisson focused on the gate that he must reach at all costs, no matter the hundred blows that would rain down upon him. He wanted to be the first to rush forward, head down, breathing in short gasps, knowing that the worst treatment would be reserved for the stragglers. He pulled with all his might on the rope so that his guard would release him and let him run as fast as he could. Again he pulled ... when, out of nowhere, his mother emerged from the crowd and rushed toward him.

Seconds later, she grabbed him by the hair and dragged him through the baying mob. They lashed out at him. Katari took a blow to the shoulder and, in her shrill voice, began to shower those around her with words of abuse that Radisson barely understood. She shouted and cursed her assailants with all her strength. Three warriors were about to strike her again when Garagonké's powerful voice boomed out over the commotion, ordering them to step back and out of the way. Grudgingly they did as he said. Katari seized the opportunity to stride forward, as a young man attacked Radisson from behind. Garagonké waved his fist at him, moved him out of the way, and rushed after his wife to protect her. The crowd turned away from them and started to beat the other prisoners, who were trying to make the most of the diversion to slip into the village.

Katari, Radisson, and Garagonké ran to seek shelter in the longhouse of the Bear clan. Safe at last, Radisson could not believe he was back among his adoptive family. That his parents had stood up for him like that was more than he ever could have hoped for. His head still spinning, he couldn't believe he'd managed to escape a beating so easily and listened with sadness as Garagonké angrily called him a traitor and a fool, reminding him how good his parents had been to him. Raising his hands skyward, holding his head, then pointing at his adopted son, he showered Radisson with insults in Iroquois. Through the stream of incomprehensible words, Radisson managed to make out that his father wanted to know why he had acted as he did, why he had killed three of his brothers and run away. Radisson jumped at the chance and responded as best he could, without the slightest trace of remorse for the cursed Algonquin who had led him right to the brink of disaster.

"I didn't kill anyone!" he exclaimed. "My brothers from the Wolf clan and I met an Algonquin while we were out hunting.

He was from the Tortoise clan, but in another village. We trusted him and shared a meal. But, in the middle of the night, he woke me up and killed my three friends before my eyes. He threatened to kill me too, unless I followed him. I didn't do anything, father! I swear to you! It was him! We fled in a canoe he had hidden in the woods. We risked our lives travelling by night. During the day we stayed hidden, too afraid to move or eat. Father, believe me! I cried bitter tears to mourn my lost brothers, but I didn't shed a tear when the Iroquois killed the hateful Algonquin! I didn't kill anyone, father! I swear!"

Radisson wasn't able to express himself as he would have wished: he couldn't always find the right words in Iroquois. But his father, now calm, seemed to have understood the gist of it all. He was deep in thought. Radisson used the opportunity to beg his mother for forgiveness. But the five warriors who had brought Radisson back to the village suddenly burst into the longhouse. They were still wearing their threatening war paint and pointed their muskets, tomahawks, and knives at him. The man who appeared to be their chief told Garagonké in no uncertain terms that he had no right to their prisoner. Garagonké knew it. Resigned, he lowered his eyes and turned away. The warriors seized Radisson and marched him to the centre of the village with the other prisoners who had survived the beating. There they bound him to a stake in the ground, along with the five men and two women. All were to be tortured. Radisson realized that his time had come. There was no one left to help him. The Iroquois from the Wolf clan would exact their revenge.

Hours later, after much chanting, dancing, and suffering, Radisson thought he was almost saved. The Algonquin at his side had his flesh seared with firebrands. Further on, a Frenchman was screaming bloody murder as his torturers lowered a necklace of red-hot tomahawk heads down onto his body. But during the whole time, only two old men came to tear out the four remaining fingernails of Radisson's right hand. He managed not to cry out. His hand now looked enormous to him, bigger than the rest of his body, throbbing and painful. But he didn't give in. He could not give in. He had to keep his head held high. To stand up to those fearless Iroquois and prove he was their equal. Radisson thanked God he did not have to suffer worse torments as children threw tiny darts at him, barely piercing his skin. He was in pain, but his life was not in danger. He could not understand why the Iroquois were going easy on him.

At the end of the long day, three young men each grabbed a firebrand and brushed the glowing branches against his face. One of them rubbed it across his chest. His chest hair went up in flames immediately, filling the air with the pungent smell of burning skin. Radisson couldn't breathe. His thoughts vanished, driven away by the all-consuming pain he must endure. He was given a few moments' respite. The pain lessened; at last he could breathe again. Later, he was taken down from the stake and brought to a longhouse he had never been inside of before. It was dark. Night had fallen. Radisson could not see a thing. There they left him alone, standing in a large empty space, hands and feet still bound.

Why did they bring him here, he wondered. Why another lull? Why was no one guarding him? The questions charged to and fro in his mind. Was his execution drawing near? Was an executioner going to finish him off at any moment with a tomahawk to the head? But nothing happened. Radisson was still awash with pain, in mortal danger. But amid the unbearable silence, the pause might be a good sign, he hoped. He clung to the fact that he hadn't been tortured as severely as the others. His will to live would help him survive this ordeal. Suddenly, he began shaking like a leaf from cold and fear. He lost hold of his emotions for a moment, afraid he was going to fall down from exhaustion onto his bleeding hand, fall onto his burning chest, cry out with fear and pain. It passed. A moonbeam feebly lit up the entrance to the longhouse, illuminating the pillars that supported the wooden frame. He wanted to get over there, lean against them, rest against them. At a snail's pace, he shuffled over, careful to keep his balance. Relief!

Wrought with pain, Radisson could not sleep, but he did find a little energy in the post he leaned against. Dazzling images exploded and flashed in his head like lightning. The painted faces of his executioners, the beloved faces of his family, memories of France, visions of torture. How sorry he was he ever came to New France. He should have stayed in Paris. He would give anything to go back and stay with his sister Marguerite, and keep his promise this time. He held his mother Katari in his arms, kind gentle Katari who abhorred torture. He prayed in the Jesuit chapel in Trois-Rivières, implored Jesus, Mary, and Joseph, and all the Holy Family. A stream of emotions. Shattered body. Liquid thoughts. His very being was breaking up.

In the early hours of the morning, the Iroquois came for him. Once again they tied him to the torture stake. It seemed as though they were ready to start all over again. A terrible weariness washed over young Radisson. All hope disappeared. This would be the day he died.

Katari sought him out and gave him a faint hope, and something to eat and drink. Before she left, she whispered in his ear: "Be brave, my son. You will not die." The words filled him with joy and drove away the pain for a moment. Then an old man came and stood beside him. With slow, deliberate movements, he prepared a tobacco pipe, lighted it, and plunged Radisson's thumb into the smouldering bowl, sucking in air greedily. Radisson's entire body was set ablaze. Immense pain flowed over his body from head to toe, devastating his thoughts, overwhelming his heart, burning his memories to a cinder. Radisson was nothing more than a ball of fire, a flame lost in the universe. Then he heard the old man telling him to sing. Radisson mustered his strength and sang, vaguely conscious of the agony of the man beside him as hot sand was poured over his head. Sickening smoke rose up from his body as he died. Radisson's voice gave out when he could sing no more, and another torturer forced him to drink an invigorating herbal tea that stirred his mind. Again he sang, sang for his life.

With the old man gone, Radisson was alone with the endless pain that had taken hold of him. It was devastating, emptying him of all substance.

At the end of this second day of torment, at sunset, Radisson saw an angry young warrior appear before him, brandishing a red-hot sword. After a few threatening thrusts, he plunged it mercilessly into Radisson's right foot. The searing pain that Radisson felt seemed scarcely harder to bear than what he was already enduring. The only thing he was still capable of thinking was that he must not cry out. He succeeded, but half lost consciousness. All that remained of his life, of his mind, of his will to live was a nightmare in which he convinced himself to suffer without crying out. He must survive one more minute, just one more minute, survive…

Radisson's mother and sisters came to comfort him. He barely sensed their presence, but was moved at the thought that human beings still wished him well. When his father joined them, a spark of joy brought momentary comfort to his aching heart. They exhorted him to stay strong while they tried to spare his life. There was hope, it seemed. "Please, free me from this suffering!" Radisson wanted to cry out. But not a sound left his mouth. When his family left, he slid back into oblivion, the words of the Jesuit missionaries ringing in his mind: "Sinners will atone for their sins in the torments of hell for all eternity." Since he had killed, God would send him to suffer in hell for all eternity. Despair.

As Iroquois custom dictated, Garagonké and Katari did everything in their power to make amends for Radisson's transgression. Katari was convinced he would never have killed his young companions. She knew him well and believed his version of events. She was sure the Algonquin must have murdered the three of them. Garagonké also believed this version. Since he was born into the Wolf clan, he had much more influence over his extended family. Ganaha had also been sent for, since he had been the first to believe in Radisson's merit and to choose him as a brother. He might be able to swing the balance in his favour. Katari and Garagonké had lost their eldest son Orinha in battle the previous year and another son, Ongienda, just recently. They had their hearts set on adopting Radisson to replace them. Most thought they deserved to keep their adopted son if that was their wish.

But negotiations were not easy. A few members of the Wolf clan were insisting on vengeance and compensation. "Why spare the life of a Frenchman? They are our enemies!" some said. Not to mention that the death of this one Frenchman would only begin to make up for the loss of the three young Iroquois he had been with. Sparing Radisson might anger the spirits of the ancestors and lead to more sorrow, others said. But Katari was resolute. Losing two sons had been painful. But she did not want to see an innocent man die, a promising young man she believed in. So she fought, she argued, she insisted, and Garagonké supported her.

THE NEXT DAY, at dawn, the ropes that held Radisson prisoner were cut. He fell immediately to the ground, then was picked up and carried into a longhouse where around fifty people had gathered. Two Iroquois took care of him, sat him down on the ground, and gave him a bitter herbal tea to drink to bring him around. Radisson wondered what was happening. Before him, old men smoked their pipes in silence. After waiting for what seemed like an eternity, he recognized his father in the middle of the crowd, smoking with the others. Garagonké was wearing two long pearl necklaces and two wampums, and from time to time he stole a glance at his adopted son. Radisson realized that he was still alive, in his Iroquois village, and not in hell.

Seven or eight other prisoners—men, women, and children—were gathered behind him. A long series of speeches began in the Iroquois language. In turn, the elders expressed themselves expansively. Radisson did not understand a word. His pain was still too intense, his fatigue too great. Then silence fell over the longhouse and, suddenly, without warning, an old woman and two children were struck once over the head with a club. They died instantly. Radisson jumped as all the other prisoners were freed in a sudden flurry of activity. He was the only prisoner not to be executed or freed.

Garagonké, Katari, and Ganaha rose to their feet and stood in front of the assembly. Radisson was overcome with joy when he saw his brother Ganaha dancing and singing with his father and mother. Radisson hadn't seen Ganaha since he had run away, and knowing Ganaha was there filled him with hope. He watched his family closely, keeping an eye on their every move. Soon his mother stopped dancing. She lifted one of the magnificent wampums from around Garagonké's neck and placed it on the ground. Then she took the other necklace, laid it across Radisson's shoulders, and the whole family stepped back. The elders whispered among themselves and from time to time threw a handful of tobacco on the fire. The wait was unbearable for Radisson, who understood nothing of the ritual. Suddenly one of the elders motioned with his hand and hundreds of people lifted up the bark walls of the longhouse. Garagonké, Katari, and Ganaha reappeared, accompanied by Radisson's two sisters. Garagonké went over to Radisson, took the wampum from his shoulders, and threw it at the feet of one of the elders. He said a few solemn words and cut the ropes that still bound Radisson's hands. Then he helped him up, telling him to rejoice for he had been saved. He was a free man: the Iroquois had forgiven him!

Radisson could barely believe it. Dizzy at the sheer joy that took hold of every fibre of his being, he found in an instant an extraordinary upsurge of energy that let him forget all his suffering. His Iroquois mother and father had given him back his life. He felt as though it was the very first day of life in the world. His heart exploded with overwhelming gratitude toward his parents. He sang in a powerful voice with his father, then hurried over to Katari to kiss her and hold his brother tight in his arms. Dozens of Iroquois sang and danced with them. The murder he committed—as though it never happened! His unforgivable actions—forgotten! The Iroquois spirits had produced a miracle!

Radisson could feel a whole new life coursing through his veins. He intended to take the opportunity granted to him to atone for his mistakes. In every fragment of his being, he was happy and proud to be an Iroquois, like his father, his mother, and all those who had pardoned him. "How sublime are Iroquois customs!" Radisson thought to himself as he sang his rediscovered happiness at the top of his voice, promising himself he would be worthy of his magnanimous parents. It was the happiest day of his life!

CHAPTER 5

BECOMING AN IROQUOIS

TWO MONTHS HAD PASSED since Radisson was tortured; at last he had fully recovered. Right after his pardon, his mothers and sisters applied plasters made from crushed plants and roots that quickly healed his wounds. Only the nails on his right hand and his pierced foot took all that long to heal.

Fall was now well underway. Nearly all the men had returned from the war and devoted their time to hunting and fishing before winter came. Some of them also went on a trading expedition to the Dutch outpost that lay four or five days' walk from the village. They brought back cloth, wool blankets, iron tomahawks and knives, and also gunpowder and muskets, leaving the Dutch beaver pelts in exchange.

In the longhouse of the Bear clan, the atmosphere was much changed. Eighty people lived there permanently. Activity was intense as preparations for winter were in full swing. Long sheaves of corn hung from outside every longhouse in the village. The women spent their days pounding dried corn kernels to make meal, which they stored in big bark containers. They also harvested squash and beans from the fields. Meanwhile the men tended several fires, which they smothered with dead leaves until they began to smoke, then hung meat and fish over them to dry so that they would last the winter. All these provisions they stored in the longhouses, laying them out on the ground or hanging them from the ceiling. To prevent the dried corn from being burned or stolen, they buried some of it in the ground, in caches lined with bark. Finally, they stocked up on firewood and repaired all the longhouses, to keep out the snow and the cold over the winter months.

His injuries meant that Radisson could hardly help with the preparations. Even had he wanted to, he lacked the Iroquois' expertise and had first to watch them closely if he were to learn. Not being able to make himself more useful made him anxious and impatient. He was eager to prove his worth to his parents. But he kept his head down, asked nothing of anyone, and thanked them profusely every time his mother and sisters tended his wounds or Ganaha taught him about hunting, fishing, and the rudiments of war. Radisson's only goal in life was to learn how to become a good Iroquois but, like a child taking baby steps, he wanted to progress much faster. Changing cultures was no mean feat.

One day, Katari decided that her son had fully recovered and encouraged him to take part in the clan's activities. For the first time, she gave him permission to go hunting with Ganaha. Radisson felt great relief: at last, his real life as an Iroquois was beginning. It would be up to him now, up to him to show what he could do, to prove himself worthy of his pardon.

And so, one fine, crisp day in November 1652, Ganaha took him hunting with Gerontatié, a cousin from the Bear clan. After half a day's walk to the south, all three lay in wait. There wasn't much game so close to the village, but Ganaha wanted to go easy on his brother's foot. Despite their patience and vigilance and a few encouraging signs of big game, the three companions only managed to kill a hare on the first two days of the expedition. But hope kept them going, perseverance being the most important quality of any hunter. On the evening of the second day, faced with such a disappointing haul, Ganaha stood at some distance from the campfire for a long while and consulted with his guardian spirit, the spirit he had chosen when he became an adult, the spirit that watched over him. He returned to his companions with a broad grin: "Tomorrow we will find what we are looking for," he said. "Now I know where to go. But we must remain on our guard because the signs the spirit sent me say there will be danger."

The next day, all three got up early and made their way stealthily to the south, eyes peeled for the slightest trace of game. Curiously, Ganaha did not examine the ground as he had on previous days. He was waiting for an animal to leap out at them without warning. And that was exactly what happened: just as they reached the top of a low hill, they found themselves face to face with a huge bear. "There it is! Shoot!" cried Ganaha, opening fire on the animal with his musket. Gerontatié fired an arrow, then another, then another with impressive speed. But the bear was charging at them as though nothing had happened. Radisson took aim, waited for the bear to draw closer, and hit it right between the eyes—just as it was about to leap at them! Ganaha had already raised his tomahawk to fight the animal, but it fell at their feet, struck down by the musket ball Radisson had lodged in its brain.

The three men stood rooted to the spot for a moment, stunned but happy to have escaped the fury of this king of the woods. Then, they started to stamp their feet with joy, dancing all around their extraordinary catch. It was the biggest bear Ganaha and Gerontatié had ever seen. That evening, they stuffed themselves with the delicious meat and sang merrily, long into the night. Once he had bedded down, Radisson could not sleep from his excitement. "It's a good omen," he repeated to himself again and again. "It's a good omen. I am Orinha, brother to Ganaha, son of Garagonké and Katari. I am a good hunter. I am Orinha. May the Iroquois spirits always be with me!"

The next morning at sunrise the three men cut the enormous animal up into three chunks and hauled it back to the village, dragging the pieces of meat behind them with ropes. When they arrived, as was the custom, they offered the meat to Katari and to Gerontatié's mother. But the mother of the Bear clan, grandmother to all the mothers in their longhouse, decided otherwise for it was she who ultimately determined where food for her clan ended up. Since the bear was an exceptional catch and there seemed to be plenty of it to go around, she wanted the meat to be shared among all clan members in a feast. Her decision was inspired by a dream she had had the night before the three hunters returned, which revealed to her that the enormous bear was a sign from the spirits. The meat would keep the whole clan strong, a clan that had once again been struck down by strange and devastating illnesses, as with every season when they traded with the Dutch. And so Radisson's first hunting expedition ended with a huge celebration and hope for the whole community. Outwardly, he appeared modestly pleased, but inside he was ecstatic.

WINTER HAD COME. Snow was building up on the bark roofs between the village dwellings, and in the forest. Soon, a few experienced groups of Iroquois hunters would leave to hunt moose for several weeks, far to the north and the east of the village. But for the time being, the men spent almost all their time around the fire, smoking and recalling war expeditions from the summer and previous years. Radisson could see how much their military exploits meant to the men in his community. Their talents and skills as hunters did not count for much in these endless discussions. The highest honour went to the victors; those who killed foes or brought prisoners back to the village. Others made much of the difficulties they overcame on their travels or laid out in great detail their battles against countless, hard-as-nails enemies to explain why they had no sought-after victories to their name. Always seated a little bit behind the others, because he had no such tales of his own to tell, Radisson listened closely to the stories. He was still too young to be a true warrior. In any case, hardly anyone showed the slightest interest in him, apart from Ganaha, who one day used him as an example as he recounted his expedition to Trois-Rivières. He told of how the two young Frenchmen accompanying Radisson were killed by warriors from the Bear clan, as he and his brother followed Radisson for an entire day, before capturing him and taking him back to the village to adopt him.

"I saw his courage when he went on alone," said Ganaha, in a loud voice. "I saw his skill when he killed ten geese with two shots of his musket. I saw his cunning when he tried to give us the slip by hiding in the woods. Despite the long journey and despite the danger he sensed, I admired his determination as he hauled all the game he killed right back to the gates of Trois-Rivières. Ongienda and I were watching him all that time and he suspected as much."

The fifteen men around the fire listened attentively to Ganaha's story. Radisson was amazed to discover that he'd been right to feel as though someone had been watching him that day. He was surprised to hear the account of that fateful day, the day his whole life changed, without feelings of regret or remorse. He had changed so much since then.

"On the way back here, I could see his desire to be at one with us. I saw he was a skilled fisherman and I saw his joy at sharing his catch with us. I saw his strength when he got the better of that arrogant Tangouen from the village of Sacandaga, who thought he was going to teach us a thing or two. And you all know how brave he was under torture. Not a peep out of him. Not a moan or a groan. He proved he was one of us. I'm telling you, my brother Orinha will be a great warrior. Give him time and we will all see his worth. Our family found solace in him when we lost our beloved brothers Orinha and Ongienda in combat. Long live Orinha!"

"Ho!" shouted the men to show their approval and give encouragement to Orinha, whom they now knew and were accepting more and more each day.

A little surprised at how he wanted to become a warrior, in line with Ganaha's plans for him, Radisson simply nodded his head in thanks. Now, such was his wish. If he had to become a warrior to earn the esteem of the Iroquois, to be loved and appreciated, then so be it. As for the two friends whose death he had just been reminded of, it all seemed so long ago that it was almost as if it had happened in a different life, as if someone else had ventured outside the stockade with François and Mathurin that day. Since then, the Iroquois had almost killed him and his life had taken a new turn. He had become Orinha and he couldn't have been happier. He had been given a second chance.

KATARI OFTEN VISITED a man from the Bear clan who seemed highly respected by his own. He lived apart from the others and rarely participated in the gatherings where everyone so enjoyed recounting their exploits. He lived at the entrance to the longhouse and spent hours on end meditating in the area set aside for his family. Radisson was curious to learn who he was and asked his mother about him.

"He is our peace chief," Katari replied. "Teharongara is the best negotiator in the Bear clan. He is the best at finding compromises and brokering alliances. He lives by the entrance to our longhouse so that each visitor may be welcomed in peace. But nobody listens to him any more. Nobody turns to him now. Since we wiped out the Hurons and the Dutch started giving us all those thunderbolts that kill, our men think only of war. But Teharongara knows a day will come when we will again have to turn to him. Even the fiercest warriors know that too."

Radisson knew that his mother was an advocate of peace. He owed his life to her. But Teharongara was a man and, judging by what he had seen, Iroquois men went to war, not least of whom his father, a respected war chief. The more Radisson learned about Garagonké, the more he admired him, the more he wanted to please him and be like him, a man who had stood up to countless foes and won many remarkable battles, the scars of which covered his whole body.

"See this scar?" Garagonké asked him one day, as he was regaling him with tales of heroic deeds. "It's round because a musket ball passed right through my arm, years ago, when I was fighting the French. And this one, this one, and this one? They are the marks of arrows that pierced my chest and thigh. I was young back then and they healed in no time. But this one on my shoulder, this long scar comes from a lance a Susquehannock warrior planted in my body. I was weak and in pain, but I still managed to kill him. I could have died right there and then. But, as you can see, I survived all these injuries, and others too that never left a mark. And each time, I would pick up my weapons again with even more courage and determination. Each time, the spirits continued to support me in combat and I vanquished my enemies. Look at the nineteen marks on my thigh. I cut them myself with my knife, one for each of the men I killed with my own hands. Your father is a courageous warrior, Orinha. You can be proud of me, just as one day I hope to be proud of you for your victories in battle. Just as I was proud of Orinha, the eldest son whose place you are taking in my heart."

Teharongara looked sad and lonely whenever Radisson saw him. His father, on the other hand, was happy and influential. He preferred to follow in the footsteps of his father, a wise, powerful, and courageous man.

IN THE HEART OF WINTER, feasts abounded in the Bear clan longhouse, as in the other village longhouses. Most paid tribute to the warriors who were making preparations for new offensives as soon as spring arrived. At these feasts, shouts, cries, dancing, and the incredible sound of drums shook the great bark structures to their foundations. The men acted out the battles they would have, leaping fearlessly over the fires that burned in the centre of the longhouses. On such occasions, Garagonké would brandish his war tomahawk, encouraging all the young men present to sow terror to the ends of the earth.

"We'll attack the Algonquins who betrayed the Iroquois!" he roared. "We'll decimate them, like we annihilated the Hurons! Both deserve the same fate for turning against our prophet Deganawida. They must perish for refusing to become one people with us, together beneath the tree of peace!"

At one such feast, after repeating his usual eloquent speech, Garagonké turned to Ganaha and said, solemnly:

"My son, the time has come for you to go to war without your father. You will go south, and I will go north. Have courage, because your honour is my honour, the honour of our family, the honour of all our clan. The whole nation is counting on us. You will sow terror among the nations to the south while I sow terror among the nations to the north. I will go and destroy the Algonquins and the French. You will go and strike fear into the lands of the Erie and the Susquehannocks. You will shake the ground to its core and save our people! Because time is of the essence, my son! Take your tomahawk and go to war! Avenge the deaths of your brothers and sisters! And avenge my own if I do not return alive from the land of the French!"

Radisson listened with fascination to his father's impassioned speech. At once moved and troubled by the calls to destroy his former people and their allies, his heart nevertheless leaned in favour of the Iroquois. This was now his family, his people, his way. But he did not really know who Deganawida was or why time was short. These questions spun around and around in his head for days, until he summoned up the courage to ask Garagonké. As though struck by his son's ignorance, his father sat up, put down the pipe he had been smoking by the fire and, after a long pause, replied:

"My son, you who have chosen to be an Iroquois, are asking essential questions. Listen well. Deganawida is our prophet. It is he who guided us along the path to union. Before Deganawida, the five Iroquois nations were at war and threatening to destroy each other. Deganawida had a vision of a tree of peace under which all the nations must come together. He advocated reconciliation and managed to bring an end to our fratricidal wars. He united our five nations and made us stronger. He also gave us the rules that govern our confederacy, the Iroquois League, bringing together the Mohawks, Oneida, Onondaga, Cayuga, and Seneca. Since he handed down these sacred rules, we settle our disputes through words and negotiation, according to his teachings, which make us more powerful every day. It is here that we Iroquois draw the strength that makes us superior to other nations.

"That's why our confederacy must now expand to take in all the nations of the earth, as Deganawida predicted. The Iroquois have opened their arms to many peoples, but some of them have pushed us away," continued Garagonké. "Several nations have refused to come together and follow the path traced by our prophet. They have chosen to become our enemies rather than sit with us beneath the big tree of peace. Our duty is to fight these nations and overcome them.

"Orinha, my son, time is short: the invaders from across the salty sea are decimating our people with their strange illnesses. The misfortune they bring with them is sowing devastation among our people and among other nations that live far from here. We must carry out our mission as soon as we can, before the evil spirits destroy us all. The Iroquois alone can overcome this terrible threat, thanks to the rules that have had us live in peace and harmony for generations. It is up to us to struggle to the very end to impose these worthy rules while there is still time. You too, my son, you can help us with our mission. I am counting on you."

The conversation filled Radisson with inspiration. From then on, every night, he dreamed of accompanying his brother Ganaha to war. He saw himself fighting and conquering enemy nations. But when he awoke, doubt again undermined his confidence and conviction. He looked at Katari and wondered who was right. She or his father? Peace or war? He feared that his mother would stand in his way and force him to stay in the village. Perhaps his father would think him too young; perhaps he would ask him to wait until he had become battle-hardened. After all, he still wasn't even allowed to go trade with the Dutch alongside the other members of his clan. What's more, he realized he would never be able to fight the French. He simply could not do it. But, night after night, his dream came back to him so powerfully and consistently that all his doubts gradually faded away. The Iroquois put great stock in dreams and now he too was set on fulfilling his destiny, his dream, his obsession. He wanted to go off to fight the Erie alongside Ganaha. He devised a plan to convince his mother and father to let him go.

ON A RADIANT day in February, Garagonké returned happy as could be from the Dutch with a couple of tomahawks, a beautiful musket, and abundant ball and powder. Radisson took advantage of his good humour to put his plan into action.

"Father, you know I am an Iroquois. You know that I love my father, my mother, and all my family. So please let me go and avenge the people of my nation. Please let me go to war with Ganaha! I want to risk my life by his side out of love for the people who have adopted me. I will fight the nations of the south with Ganaha. The enemies I kill will make my father proud. The prisoners I bring back will make my mother happy. I will prove to you that I am the equal of the son Orinha that you lost. I will be as courageous, as brave, as valiant as he. You will see; I am worthy of the name you have given me. I am ready to die for my family and my nation! I beg you, father, let me go to war with Ganaha!"

Upon hearing these words, Garagonké jumped to his feet and cried out with joy.

"Orinha, you have returned, my son! Take courage, for the man you are replacing in my heart died in battle and not at home like a woman. Orinha was brave and daring. He died in combat outnumbered ten to one. So, yes, since that is what you desire, you too may go off to war. Go with Ganaha! You will avenge my two sons who fell in combat, and make me happy! Rejoice, my son, because the time has come for you to prove what you are made of."

LESS THAN ONE MOON later, the Bear clan held a feast to mark the departure of the first war party of the year. Katari tried to keep her son at home, on the pretext that he was too young to undertake such a perilous journey, but in vain. Garagonké decided such matters and Radisson had convinced him he was ready.

Members of the Tortoise clan were invited to the feast as the leader of the war party, Kondaron, was from their clan. The previous summer, he had undertaken a victorious campaign against the Erie, making him the obvious choice to lead Ganaha, Radisson, and the six other warriors from the Bear clan that made up the troop. This time Radisson joined in the dancing and shouted out the war song he had chosen, delighted at the chance to show the Iroquois his strength and enthusiasm. He got to know Kondaron, his captain: a young warrior who was both bigger and stronger than he was, twenty-three years old, just like Ganaha. He made a powerful impression. Despite his youth, Kondaron's face, gestures, and words already showed the confidence and dignity of an older, more experienced man. Kondaron promised Garagonké he would do everything in his power to protect his two sons, kill as many enemies as possible, and bring back many prisoners.

After a copious meal prepared in huge copper cooking pots acquired from the Dutch, after the singing, the dancing, and the shows of strength from the nine young warriors, Radisson's father took the floor to bring the evening to a close.

"My heart is heavy at having to wait for another whole moon

before I myself leave for war against the nations in the north, where winter still lingers on. But I am glad to see the first war party of the year go out, and gladder still to celebrate the determination shown by my two sons, to whom I wish courage and success. Kondaron will make a fine war chief: powerful spirits have guided and protected him since he was born. I implore the spirits of our ancestors to help you show once and for all the supremacy of the Iroquois over all other nations. Hail Kondaron, Ganaha, Orinha, Otasseté, Tahonsiwa, Shononses, Tahira, Deconissora, and Thadodaho, who will sow terror among the Erie!"

Katari did not shout with joy along with others. Sitting a bit toward the rear, with her friend Teharongara, the peace chief, she was disappointed to see Orinha become a warrior so quickly and so readily. She had hoped he would help her advocate for peace, which she believed to be more and more vital to the well-being of her clan and her family. But Orinha was lost to the war fever for that had taken hold of the entire Mohawk nation. She did not feel much like celebrating.

Conharassan, Orinha's favourite sister, also shed a tear as she expressed her lukewarm enthusiasm. She had distanced herself from her brother ever since he had returned to the village, ever since the three young men he had left with had been murdered, since he had run away, since he had been tortured and pardoned. The affair was still on everybody's lips, and some of the rumours divided her loyalties. Some said Radisson really had murdered the Iroquois. But in spite of everything, she still loved this man. He was not like anyone else she knew, and she was sad to see him go.

|||||||||||||||||||||||||||||||||||||||||||||||||||||||||||||||||||||||||||||||||||||||||||||||||||||||

CHAPTER 6

ORINHA, APPRENTICE WARRIOR

O N A WARM SPRING DAY, the small troop left the village. Radisson and each of his eight companions carried a musket, ample supplies of powder and shot, a tomahawk, an iron knife, two shirts, a coat, and two wool blankets—all obtained from their Dutch neighbours in exchange for beaver pelts. They also each brought eight pairs of leather moccasins for the trail ahead, which looked like being long indeed, and two pieces of leather cut in advance from which to make a new pair of pants, when the time came. They had a good reserve of cornmeal for times when hunting and fishing would bring scant reward, and for luck each wore a precious wampum, the shell necklaces so prized by the Iroquois. If need be, they could trade them to get out of a tight spot.

Radisson looked just like his companions in every respect: head shaved for combat with only a thin strip of hair down the middle, weather-beaten skin, shell necklace and bracelet. With his sturdy shoulders, broad chest, and muscular legs, he was built like a bear, only taller: in fact, he was one of the tallest in the group. The red, black, and brown war paint he was wearing masked the firm lines of his smiling face. His black, piercing eyes gleamed with joy now that he had won the confidence of his family, of his clan, and was getting ready to fulfill his dream: he was off to discover wide-open spaces and live a life of adventure. At last he would be able to prove to his parents that they were right to forgive him and take him in as their own son. He felt he was Orinha from the tips of his hair to the ends of his fingernails and promised himself to accomplish the exploits everyone expected of him.

His group strode out of the village to the cheers of dozens of members of the Bear clan. Radisson did not look back. The farewell ceremonies were over, and the future now lay before of him. He had only to follow Ganaha and their chief Kondaron to fulfill his destiny as a warrior. When he returned from this campaign, he was quite sure he would have repaid his debt to his parents and his Iroquois brothers.

WHEN THEY REACHED the land of the Oneida, the Mohawks' immediate neighbours, a warrior by the name of Atotara, who was even younger than Radisson, joined the group. He had fought the previous fall alongside Ganaha, who had promised to bring him on his next campaign. All except Kondaron were from the Bear clan, and the clan was organizing a big feast to celebrate the party's departure. Radisson was pleased at no longer being the youngest and sang and danced so energetic- ally at the feast that Atotara's family and friends were filled with admiration. Carried away by his enthusiasm, he told any- one who cared to listen how many enemies he would kill and how many prisoners he would bring back. Everyone congratu- lated him, especially Kondaron and Ganaha, and the Oneida were delighted that an adopted Frenchman had joined their cause with such relish.

The ten warriors cut across the lands of the Onondaga, the Cayuga, and then the Seneca, moving steadily westward. They were welcomed everywhere they went with just as much warmth and enthusiasm. The fighting season would soon begin for all. With every passing village, Radisson felt more at ease in his new role as warrior. Following his companions' example, he promised time and again to shake the Erie nation to its foundations and return victorious.

Once they passed the last Seneca village, once the slaves they brought with them set down their packs and turned back along with the Seneca that had come along to encourage them, the festive fever evaporated. The ten warriors found themselves alone, ready to begin a long journey and encounter dangers and obstacles that were shaping up to be plentiful. Kondaron paused before their long journey really began and gave a speech to spur on each of his men, who stood gathered in a circle around him.

"We are now going to take the route I followed last year," he told them. "It is long and will sometimes be difficult. But I know it well and I know how to work around the obstacles we will encounter. I am sure it will lead us on to victory: never has a chief been able to count on so many fearless warriors as I. To win, my brothers, every day we must remind ourselves that we need each other like the soil needs the rain and the sun if it is to grow corn. Whatever the obstacles, we will overcome them. Whatever the enemies, we will fight together as a single man. And we will all return to this place and celebrate our victories. Do not forget, Ganaha, I am counting on you. Just as I am counting on you, Otasseté, Tahonsiwa, and Shononses, just as much as I am counting on Tahira, Deconissora, and Thadodaho. Orinha and Atotara, you are the youngest among us and you have not yet known real battle. I am also counting on you. We are all in this great adventure together. We are all a single being. Now, take your packs and follow me. We will walk for days to reach a huge lake. The Erie live at the end of the lake. Let us be off, my brothers! May the spirits be with us!"

"Ho! Ho!" the men called out as one, to show they were behind Kondaron.

Ganaha realized it was now his duty to keep an eye on Orinha. His younger brother still had much to learn about war and travel through unknown territory. He began to give him advice.

"Put your snowshoes on first," he told him. "Then pick up your pack. Adjust the strap to balance the weight on your back. Don't lean too far forward, or too far back. Find your balance... Ready? Follow me."

Radisson, the least experienced member of the group, took longer than the others to get ready. He and Ganaha hurried to catch up with their companions, but Radisson was carrying a heavy load, and constantly slipping and sliding on the muddy ground covered with melting snow. Ganaha was by now far ahead of him and took his place at the head of the group, just behind Kondaron. Despite his best efforts, Radisson brought up the rear and fell further behind, far behind Atotara who, although not as strong, was more accustomed to walking with snowshoes. Ganaha regularly waited for his brother to catch up, encouraging him and keeping him company.

"How are you doing? Tired? Need help?"

"No!" snapped Radisson, too proud to admit he was finding the going tough. "My snowshoes need adjusting. It will be better tomorrow. Go walk with the others, at your own pace. Atotara and I will follow your tracks."

In truth, Radisson was afraid the day would never end. He did not know his companions were so strong, so tough, so indifferent to hardship. On and on they walked without ever stopping, not even to eat. They hurried ahead and Radisson had trouble keeping up with Atotara, who was now completely out of sight. At the end of the day, when he could barely make out his companions' tracks in the snow and the trees seemed to be closing in around him, towering, dark, and menacing, fear washed over him. Fortunately, Ganaha came back to meet him, and Radisson was doubly relieved. First, to see him appear around a bend, and then to learn he was only ten minutes away from camp. He'd managed to survive the first day. His honour was intact. And nobody was holding his lack of experience or the fact that he was late against him. Kondaron and Otasseté even congratulated him for managing to keep up so well. "It'll be easier tomorrow," Kondaron told him. "You'll get used to it."

Atotara was just as exhausted as Radisson and threw him an understanding glance. Both could think only of getting some rest while the others divided the work between themselves. Four of them made the most of the last glimmers of daylight to go hunting nearby. The others set up camp for the night, gathering fir tree boughs to sleep on, finding wood for the fire, and cooking what food they had. Soon they were gathered around the fire for a frugal meal.

For the next six days, from dawn to dusk, they kept up their furious pace, almost without stopping. The forest unfolded before them, slowly and endlessly. A few clumps of conifers added a dash of colour amidst the bare-leaved trees that lined the monotonous landscape with their thin branches. The only consolation was the heartening sight of the warm sun that occasionally shone in the blue sky. But the warmth made the snow heavy and sticky, and transformed their snowshoes into balls and chains they were forced to drag along behind them like condemned men. Taking them off did not help either: their feet sank deep into the snow, making walking almost impossible. Radisson, who wasn't used to walking at such a pace with snowshoes, and with so much weight on his back, often lost his footing on the half-frozen ground. He became angry with himself and hurried to catch up with the others, seething. How he wanted to know everything there was to know about the life of these Iroquois warriors! At least once a day, Ganaha left his favoured place just behind Kondaron at the head of the column to spend some time alongside Radisson.

The time spent with Ganaha was an extraordinary source of motivation for young Orinha, who was forgetting more and more that he was once Radisson. Even though he was still dead last, he could now remain a part of the group the whole day. He was pleased and proud of his progress, especially since his companions were showing more confidence in him by the day. Whenever Ganaha and Radisson walked together, they spoke very little. From time to time, his elder brother pointed out an animal scurrying back into the forest, drew his attention to a feature of the landscape that could be used as a landmark, or showed him a valuable tree and told him what it was used for. He was constantly encouraging Orinha, ensuring he made rapid progress. The weight on Orinha's shoulders seemed to grow lighter, and the forest became more fascinating, more enlightening.

At day's end, the small group busied itself finding something to eat and getting ready for bed. The routine was well established, and it was reassuring how the group's members worked together so efficiently.

WHEN THEY REACHED the broad lake they had to cross to reach the Erie, Kondaron looked visibly disappointed. Unlike the previous year, it was still frozen, and the time they would be forced to wait went against the chief's plans. On the other hand, at least they now had plenty of time to build the canoes they would need to cross the water.

On the first day, they built a bark lodge where the forest met the shore, to shelter from the cold and the bad weather. It was just big enough for all ten of them to sleep in, around a modest fire.

The next day, they began building their canoes. For want of birch, which was rare in this part of the country, the ten men paired off in search of the elms that would give them the bark they needed. Ganaha and his younger brother Orinha were on the same team.

"Look!" exclaimed Ganaha, pointing out an enormous elm, tall and straight. "No need to look any further! Let me show you how it's done." Orinha watched his brother cut a large groove around the tree with his knife, at about thigh height. Then he lifted his head and pointed out to Orinha the junction of the first big branch and the trunk, several feet above their heads.

"You climb up there," Ganaha instructed him, "and cut another groove around the tree, just above that big branch. Then, cut the bark lengthwise from top to bottom. After that, I'll show you how to peel the bark away without breaking it."

"No problem," replied Orinha. "But how do I get up there? And once I'm there, how will I find the strength to cut through the bark the way you did?"

"Don't worry. You'll manage. We'll start by building you something to stand on."

Through the thin layer of snow that still covered the forest floor, Ganaha spied two long branches. They were dead but seemed solid enough. With his tomahawk, he freed them and cut them to the right length. Then he leaned them tight against the trunk of the elm.

"Climb up these poles and stand on them. I'll help you. Then, loop this rope around your waist, and then around the tree. That way you'll have both hands free to cut into the bark with your knife. Got it?"

"Got it! I'll take a run-up and you give me a shove when I reach you, got it?"

"Got it."

"Here I come..."

Orinha dashed forward as Ganaha pushed him upward with all his strength, and all of a sudden the younger brother was standing at the top of their makeshift ladder, right where it met the trunk. Orinha hugged the tree, looped the rope around it, and then set about cutting deep into the bark, right down to the wood. The brothers moved their ladder three times as they worked their way around the tree. All they had to do now was cut the bark from top to bottom, the easiest part. Orinha grabbed the knife with both hands and put all his weight against it, letting himself slide back down into Ganaha's arms. Then his brother took care of the awkward part, slowly tearing the bark away from the trunk, careful not to let it break.

The operation took them all day. At dusk, the brothers brought the long roll of bark back to camp. It was in perfect condition and would be used to make the hull of a canoe. The next day Shononses, Otasseté, Thadodaho, and Tahira brought back two shorter rolls of bark from thinner elms.

Otasseté was the most experienced canoe builder among them. He oversaw the building of the three canoes, with help from Shononses and Thadodaho. The others cut and prepared the thin inside ribs that would make it tough and strong. Next, they dug up and prepared the roots that were used to sew the strips of bark and the wood ribs together. The last step was to make the seams watertight, using spruce gum. Eight days later, the group boasted one large canoe seating four and two smaller ones that could carry three people each.

Orinha, who was learning each of the techniques for the very first time, was impressed by his companions' ingenuity. They had come here with no materials at all, with only tomahawks and knives for tools, and now in no time at all they had three solid canoes that would bring them to the ends of the earth! His opinion of them, formed as he listened to neverending boasts of their military prowess around the fire, or watched their eyes light up at games of chance, had completely changed. Here, deep in the forest, on the warpath, his friends were revealing their many talents. Orinha was happy to be living life to the full with them.

BUILDING THE CANOES had taken their mind off the lingering bad weather. Now that they were ready to push off onto the still-frozen lake, they did not know what to do. They could not stand being crowded into their smoky camp shelter for hours on end, even though it protected them from the violent squalls that chilled their morale as much as their bodies. The cold and wind seemed to have frozen even the game, no trace of which could be found in the forest. All too often, the hunters came back empty-handed. What's more, the fragile, porous ice that still covered the lake was preventing them from moving away from the shoreline and fishing beneath the ice, as they would have done in the heart of winter. And so they were reduced to eating away at their rapidly declining provisions of cornmeal, provisions that were intended for use only in combat or on long journeys.

Kondaron was worried. He wondered if the setbacks they'd experienced meant the spirits were not favourable to the campaign. He wasn't contemplating turning back just yet, but doubt had begun to set in. Orinha, who thus far hadn't set much store by the often subtle revelations made by the spirits, could also feel the anxiety spreading throughout the war party.

One morning, a bad dream awakened Kondaron. Shaken by the images that suddenly loomed before him, he hurriedly made a fire and threw a few handfuls of tobacco into the flames to ward off the ill fortune that had appeared to him in his sleep. His surprised companions worried even more when Kondaron went off before they could share the meal Shononses had prepared for them, saying: "I must consult the spirits. Do not disturb me. I will be down by the lake." To lighten the atmosphere, Shononses shrugged and suggested they go ahead and eat, as though nothing had happened. Later, midway through an idle day when nobody felt much like doing anything, Ganaha made up his mind to seek out Kondaron, saying he wanted to go hunting. But first he hoped to find out what was on his mind. Kondaron saw him approach and spoke first:

"You were right to come."

Reassured, Ganaha sat down beside him and said:

"Good. We are worried, my brother. I came to ask why you are hiding what troubles you. Are we not all bound by the same fate?"

"The bad dream I had last night concerns but one of us," replied Kondaron.

"Orinha or Atotara?" asked Ganaha, after a moment's thought.

"Atotara is of the same blood and the same clan as we are. I mean Orinha."

"Orinha is also part of the Bear clan," Ganaha replied. "He comes from my family. He is the adopted son who has taken the place of my beloved brother. He is loved very much by Katari and Garagonké, and by me."

"You are right. But that is not what is worrying me. You forget that we don't know how he lived as a Frenchman before he became one of us. You know him better than any of us. Do you know?"

"No," admitted Ganaha. "All I know is that he showed himself to be brave and skilful when we captured him. I know he loves the Iroquois and wants to fight with us. He wants to win with us. He is sincere. Of that I have no doubt."

Kondaron's face twitched slightly at the thought of the bad dream that had awakened him up with a start. How could he read anything into it if Orinha's past remained a mystery to them? How could he comprehend the sign sent to him by the spirits? What did the image of suffering and death sent to him mean?

"I believe it too," replied Kondaron after a moment. "But that's not the issue. Last night, I saw your brother perish beneath the blows of our enemies. His body was covered in blood and pierced with arrows, a stone tomahawk planted in his head. I am wondering if that means he is to die on our campaign."

Ganaha kept silent. Now it was his turn to be troubled by the morbid image.

"Have you noticed that Orinha doesn't wear a medicine bag like the rest of us?" continued Kondaron. "Do you know if a spirit is protecting him?"

Ganaha remained deep in thought. He did not know.

"It is true that Orinha wears no visible sign of the spirit that is protecting him," he finally answered. "I don't know if young Frenchmen choose a spirit to guide them for the rest of their lives, as we do. I've never thought about it before."

"Who will protect him then when he battles at our side? You? Me? Will the power of my guardian spirit extend to him? Will the word I gave to your father and my vigilance be enough? I am wondering what to do, Ganaha."

Ganaha did not have an answer. Suddenly he was overwhelmed at the thought that an ill omen seemed to be hanging over his brother, the younger brother that he too had promised to protect. He hoped the French won the favour of the spirits in their own way, and that he and his chief would be helped by spirits they did not know. He recalled the Great Spirit the Jesuit who lived in their longhouse for a few weeks would talk about.

"Anyway," Kondaron went on, "it's up to me to resolve the problem. I'm asking you to continue to keep an eye on your brother as you've been doing. Show him everything he needs to know. I'll find a way to extend the protection of the spirits that favour us. Because the spirits are once again in our favour, my dear brother. Look over there, in the middle of the lake."

Ganaha turned his head and saw the sun glinting off the lake's surface.

"The water is starting to filter through the ice," Kondaron explained. "The pool of water reflecting the sun has been growing steadily since this morning. I've been watching it closely. Tonight, tomorrow at the latest, the ice will give way entirely and the lake will be free. And we will at last be able to paddle across to the Erie! Come, let's share the good news with our companions."

As they paddled energetically across what seemed like a sea of fresh water as big as the ocean, beneath a resplendent sun, carried along by a gentle breeze pushing them in the right direction, Orinha was drunk with happiness. When he felt thirsty, he drank clear water straight from the lake. When he was hungry, he ate the fish they'd caught that day. Each night, after setting up camp on the beckoning shore, they gathered around the fire to eat, sing, and tell stories. When night came, they slept under the stars beneath their canoes, breathing in the air perfumed with the springtime flora that was sprouting up everywhere around them. Orinha could not imagine being any happier. Nature's generosity, the simple life, the freedom, this thrilling trip that carried him ever further, all were worth all the gold in the world. He savoured every minute of their time on the water, every instant given back to him one hundred-fold after his brush with death. Life provided him with everything he could wish for. He was happy to be an Iroquois. The serene days even caused him to forget the main reason for the idyllic journey—war.

A week later, they reached the end of the lake. Kondaron chose the mouth of a broad river to set up a long-term camp.

"From now on," he explained, "our path will be less safe. We will have to be on our guard: the land of the Erie is not far away. Before we engage the enemy, we will have to stock up on provisions. Let each man get ready to hunt and fish. We will stay here for as long as it takes."

The ten men set about fishing right away. While Kondaron led four of the warriors hunting, three others stayed behind to smoke the fish they caught. Alone in his canoe, Orinha continued to fish a short distance from shore, fascinated by the immensity of the light-flooded lake. He wished the magic could last forever, that they would never turn inland to fight. He never tired of admiring the fresh vegetation that coloured the horizon, or of thanking nature for providing them with everything they needed, and more. A kind of ecstasy took hold of him as the blazing sun rose to its zenith in the pure blue sky. He was thrilled to be fishing for his brothers while they hunted for him, the same brothers who stuck together in life and in death and would soon be fighting alongside each other to save the peoples of the earth.

As in a dream, Orinha imagined himself coming to this part of the world in different circumstances, to put into action an idea that had always been dear to him. His capture had brought his plans to an abrupt end, but he could see himself returning here to trade and to experience momentous events that would turn his world upside down. The powerful sun was making him dizzy. Out on the water, its intense reflections were blinding him. He read his fate in the gentle swaying canoe atop the water, written in letters of gold, like a message from another dimension. Orinha floated across the immense lake, across time, in a parallel world where humans, spirits, animals, earth, and water lived together in harmony.

Cries rang out from the shoreline: "Orinha! Orinha! It's getting dark! Come and eat!" His companions were waving to him. His dream vanished. He realized that the sun was disappearing over the horizon in a thousand shining colours. It was time to go back. Quickly, Orinha shook himself, pulled in his lines, grabbed his paddle, and headed back to camp. Ganaha was waiting for him on the shoreline with open arms: "Look, Orinha!" he exclaimed. "Look at the huge deer we killed! We'll have enough meat for a week!"

By now they had smoked and dried more provisions than they could carry. It was time to turn inland in search of the Erie.

THE RIVER FLOWED slowly through flat terrain. They made rapid progress to the headwaters. After four days, they reached a small lake that Kondaron recognized. They were arriving in enemy territory, he told them; they must keep their wits about them. To the south and west of the crescent-shaped lake, forest fire had razed a vast area that they must cross to reach the land of the Erie. Kondaron thought it prudent to leave the canoes hidden by the lakeside, on the outskirts of that part of the forest spared by the fire, so they could make a quick escape if pursued by the enemy. If need be, they could build new ones.

They shouldered their weapons and packs and continued on their way through the wasteland. There was nothing to hide behind and they felt under constant threat. They made quick progress, raising an acrid dust that stuck in their throats and choked them. Their supply of fresh water soon ran dry and they were reduced to drinking the cloudy, ash-filled water they found in ponds and brooks. Every last animal had deserted that sterile place; the war party had to dip into its provisions of smoked meat and fish. When at last they reached the other side of the death and destruction, relieved no one had spotted them, Kondaron ordered a day of rest.

After they had rested, they came to a hilly region and there followed a turbulent river that wound its way between steep banks. Sometimes they had to take to the riverbed, wading through the water, careful to keep their powder and muskets dry. When the current got too strong, they clambered up onto the bank and walked on through the woods. They advanced in this fashion for two days, heading south through the high hills. From the top of a headland, Kondaron at last saw a welcoming river flowing through a broad valley: the land of the Erie.

Their every sense on high alert, without a sound, the ten men filed down through the open forest. Orinha was the only one to crack a twig or two underfoot. Ganaha, walking just ahead of him, turned and shot him furious glances. But all Orinha could do is shrug—there was nothing to do but wait until he became as nimble as his companions. It took them a few hours to reach the river. After carefully scrutinizing the area, Kondaron relaxed and announced that the Erie villages were still a good distance away: "We can set up camp here, no problem," he told them. "Let's retrace our steps and build a fortified camp a good distance away from the water. We'll also have to build new canoes to move around in."

They selected a site slightly higher than its surroundings for their camp, five hundred paces from the river. A few conifers provided a screen. The next day, while the more experienced men fetched the bark needed to make canoes, gathered firewood, and went off hunting Kondaron brought Orinha and Atotara with him to inspect their surroundings. They combed the riverbank for the slightest indication of human activity. Kondaron scanned the ground and searched the sky above the opposite shore for any sign of smoke that would betray the presence of the Erie. As they moved about, he was careful not to snap the tiniest twig: he nudged them out of the way with his foot, clearing himself a path to ensure no one would ever know they had passed that way. He instructed his two young warriors to do exactly as he did and to take their bearings as they went.

At the end of the day, as an exercise, Kondaron relied on his protégés to return to camp. Orinha had trouble finding the landmarks he had noted, but Atotara did it with ease. Subtly, Kondaron watched them just as carefully as he had looked for signs of life from the Erie. In both cases, he was satisfied. He'd found not a single trace of their enemy, and the war party's two youngest members appeared ready for combat.

Kondaron allowed tomahawks to be used to build the shelter and the canoes, which would be cruder than before. Hunting with a musket was the only thing he forbade: the noise would surely betray them. The log wall of the fortified camp was high enough to protect them from any Erie attack and large enough for them to sleep in safety during the night. A makeshift bark roof protected them from the elements. During the daytime, to avoid being surprised by the enemy, two men stood guard on a spit of land that jutted out into the river. When darkness fell, they all gathered around a crackling campfire. As they did not fear a night attack, they passed the time eating, talking, and loudly singing their war songs. Kondaron used the time to tell them tales of his victorious battles in the area last year. The emotion was palpable every time he mentioned the hundreds of people he terrorized with the firearms the Erie did not know, and the dozens of men and women killed or taken prisoner. "But this time," he warned, "there are fewer of us, and the Erie will be less frightened of our muskets—many of them will know of them now. No doubt they will be better prepared to fight us. We must be extremely careful. I am counting on each of you to keep us safe. Stick together and always fight together. And we will win."

The preparations over, Kondaron divided the war party into three. Each group would head out in a different direction to explore the area. That way, they would locate the enemy quickly, wherever they might be. Four warriors would go north in one of the larger canoes; four more would head south in the other. Orinha and Atotara would travel up the stream opposite the encampment in the small canoe. "We'll report back at camp at the end of the day," said Kondaron.

The stream was cluttered with fallen tree trunks, rocks, and roots, making headway difficult. Again and again they had to get out and wade through the water, dragging the canoe over obstacles. Then they jumped back in and paddled for a short distance, wading around more obstacles. Both wondered why Kondaron had sent them off in this direction, where they were sure no one ever came. But it was the mission their chief had assigned them, and they intended to fulfill it to the best of their ability.

After several hours, they at last reached a small lake upon which they were surprised to see two human forms in the distance. They had been making no attempt to be silent, so their first reflex was to dive into the undergrowth and hide, in case their enemies heard them and attacked. They quickly opened the bark container protecting their powder and loaded their muskets, ears alert to the slightest suspicious sound. Nothing out of the ordinary happened. No one seemed to have seen them. Now that they could breathe more easily, they thought about what they should do.

Atotara whispered in Orinha's ear. He wanted to climb a tree to get an idea of how many people were out on the lake and see what they were up to. Orinha agreed in a whisper: "Go ahead. But stay well hidden and don't make a sound. I'll stay down here to keep watch." Atotara climbed up onto Orinha's shoulders, then hoisted himself up from one branch to another until he'd reached the top of a tall yellow birch. He stayed there for several minutes, not moving a muscle, until Orinha heard him scampering back down. He landed on the ground with a thud and Radisson lost his temper:

"Shh!" he whispered. "You'll give us away!"

"There are only two of them," Atotara replied. "Two fishermen. There's no danger. Quick! We still have time to attack before nightfall! It will be our first victory and Kondaron will be proud of us! Follow me."

But Orinha shook his head violently.

"No!" he replied. "Stay here! If we attack with guns, the Erie will know the Iroquois are back. If any more of them are nearby, they'll attack and kill us, or else they'll warn other Erie and hunt us down. It's a stupid idea! We have to do what Kondaron said. We'll return to camp and tell everyone we have found our enemies. C'mon, let's go back!"

Now it was Atotara's turn to reject his companion's idea out of hand. They started pushing and shoving each other, but Orinha was the stronger and managed to drag Atotara back to the canoe. The younger warrior had to swallow his anger and accept the law of the strongest, however difficult it might be. But he sat at the back of the canoe and only pretended to paddle. Orinha did all the work up front.

The sun was already disappearing behind the trees. The day had gone by like a flash. No matter how hard Orinha paddled and wrestled with the obstacles in their path, the canoe could barely make headway. Atotara even refused to get out when his "chief" asked him to, stubbornly repeating: "We'd be far better off attacking them. They don't suspect a thing. It would be so easy."

"Shut up!" snapped Orinha. "We have to tell Kondaron."

"We'll bring two scalps back to camp and tell them, 'we were the first to find the Erie. Follow us.'"

"Kondaron told us to be careful and to stick together. He wants us to attack together. Don't you ever listen?"

They wasted a huge amount of time arguing back and forth. Night came and rain suddenly started to fall. The heavens opened. There was no way they could continue in such conditions. Finally, they decided to shelter on shore, protecting themselves under the overturned canoe. They had nothing to eat. And it was too late to make a fire in such a downpour. It was cold. All night long, they huddled together in their tiny shelter, furious with each other, not exchanging a word. Happily, the rain stopped at daybreak. Relieved, the two set off again on a stream swollen by the cloudburst. The current swept them along toward the river. Their good humour returned at the thought that soon they would be eating with their companions. More than anything, they couldn't wait to tell Kondaron they had found the enemy.

ALONG WITH Otasseté, Ganaha had been keeping watch since dawn on the spit of land that formed a bend in the river. He'd slept badly and, worried, peered at the brook where Atotara and his brother had disappeared the day before. They hadn't returned to camp for the night, as planned. He recalled Kondaron's dream all too well, and the threat that hung over his brother. He was annoyed at himself for letting Orinha go off with the inexperienced Atotara, however harmless the brook might have looked. It was his responsibility to keep an eye on him. He also wondered why Kondaron had sent the party's two youngest members to explore unknown territory alone in the first place.

Time passed, and Ganaha was worried sick. If Orinha hadn't already been ambushed or gotten lost in the forest, he swore he'd never let him leave his side again. After all, it was he who first saw what Orinha was made of. It was he who wanted him to join his family. And now it was up to Ganaha to make a real warrior out of him! He swore he would avenge Orinha's death if ever the Erie had killed him. He would get them!

At last! The two youngsters came into sight at the mouth of the stream, paddling feverishly toward him. Ganaha leaped out of his hiding place, waving furiously. He guided them to him, happy to see they were still alive. Otasseté remained at his post while Ganaha helped them land, then hide the canoe.

"What happened to you?" he asked anxiously.

"We found the Erie!" they cried out.

The three rushed off to give Kondaron the good news. He decided they would attack the enemy the next day. Ganaha was proud of his brother.

That evening, Kondaron went off to meditate. Before going back to his companions, he chopped down a small fir tree and cut off the top. Then, he gathered his nine warriors around the fire to tell them a story handed down to him by his father.

"One day," he began solemnly, "two young brothers got lost in the woods. They had gone hunting to feed the members of their clan. They didn't know where they were because they were so far away from their land. When night surprised them deep in the woods, far from home, they kept on going, even though they had completely lost their bearings. The next morning, they still couldn't find their way back. For days and nights on end, they wandered up hill and down dale, tormented by worry and hunger. They used up all their arrows, then they broke their bows, and even lost their tomahawks. After wandering for a whole moon, they recognized none of the lands they were travelling through. They were driven to despair. It was then that an incredibly tall old man appeared to them, the sunlight shining down brightly on his face, and spoke to them in a loud voice: 'I can bring an end to your suffering, for I am a powerful spirit. I know every animal, every plant, and every pathway in this forest. I can guide you home to your village, if you so desire. I am offering you my help because I can see that you are two brave young men, and strong too. I also have the power to grant you a long life alongside your wives and children. But first, you must eat, for the journey will be long. Take this.'"

Kondaron extended his hands to his companions, as though he were offering them something to eat. They listened on in silence.

"Well, this giant was the Great Spirit. The Great Spirit leaned toward them and offered them a bloody lump of human flesh. Seeing it, the youngest recoiled and hid his face in his hands, refusing to eat. But his older brother accepted the human flesh. To nourish the younger brother who had refused to touch the flesh of a man, the giant gave him a piece of bear meat, which he accepted readily. The meal reinvigorated the two brothers. They followed the old man's directions and soon found the path back to their village."

"The giant was a good spirit," said Kondaron. "The two brothers lived with their wives for many more years and had many children. The younger brother became a hunter renowned for the many bears he killed, while the elder brother became a famous warrior who captured and killed many men and women. The spirit had revealed their destiny to them and allowed it to come to pass."

Kondaron's story was met with a profound silence. All of Orinha's companions were familiar with the legend; most had heard it time and time again. For once, nobody followed with a story of his own, or started to sing. On the eve of combat against the Erie, all were deep in thought. Their chief's tale reminded each of them that it was time to communicate with their guardian spirits, the spirits they chose when they became adults, from among all the spirits that brought the world to life: the spirits of the beaver, the eagle, the oak tree, the reed, the earth, the water, the sun, the spirits of all that existed. Only Orinha had never experienced this. Unlike his companions, he was quietly wondering what meaning to give to the story that troubled him more than it reassured him. Who was he? A hunter or a warrior? Perhaps he was no more than a trader, as he had often thought? Perhaps he was a negotiator, a man of peace? His life had changed so quickly.

Before leaving the village, Orinha had seen Iroquois his age shut themselves away to fast and seek the spirit that would guide their destiny. After fasting, each young man would then always wear a bag made from leather or bark around his neck or waist, a bag that contained a secret talisman. None of them would ever reveal its contents. And so Orinha understood precious little about the whole thing. On that evening, he noticed that all his companions were wearing such a bag. Was it really that important? He couldn't say. But at that very minute, he felt vulnerable and very different from the other Iroquois. The thought irritated him. When his life was on the line, he wanted to be like his brothers in every respect, to form one body with them.

He was almost angry with Kondaron for choosing this moment to tell his story, even though he realized it was a source of inspiration for his comrades. What could he do to rid himself of his uncomfortable feeling? Orinha looked for solace in Ganaha's eyes, but his elder brother kept his head down, lost in thought. To perk up his courage, Orinha recalled Garagonké's enthusiasm when he told him he wanted to go to war. The memory comforted him a little.

Kondaron beckoned Orinha to follow him outside the walls of the camp. Once they were a few steps away, in the flickering light of the fire, Kondaron gave him a small bark cylinder, sewn together at both ends with roots through which long leather thong had been threaded. Kondaron knotted it solemnly around Orinha's waist, saying:

"This talisman will protect you for the entire journey. You must trust its power. The spirit that lives in it is powerful enough to watch over both you and me. It is part of my own spirit. You must never open it and you must not know what it contains. All I can tell you is that this spirit lives in the sky like the Great Spirit of the French, and his anger is terrible. But his power is also on our side, especially in battle. I ask you to respect him and to always be careful not to anger him. May the spirit be with you. You have nothing to fear any more."

So saying, Kondaron went back to sit by the fire without further explanation. Orinha rushed after him, hoping to question him.

"How can I respect him if I don't know who he is? Tell me, Kondaron. Tell me more. Tell me what I have to do."

But the chief remained silent. He now gazed sternly at the fire and threw a few handfuls of tobacco onto it. They disappeared into the air as smoke.

"Tell me how to pray to him, how to worship him," Orinha insisted. "Please teach me."

Kondaron said not a word. But Ganaha noticed the bark cylinder tied around his brother's waist and smiled over at Orinha, relieved that Kondaron had found a way to protect him. "You must rest," Kondaron finally declared. "Sleep well, for tomorrow we will need all our strength. Put your faith in the spirits—they are on our side. You have nothing to fear."

But that night Orinha had too many questions to be able to sleep. He nervously touched the bark cylinder Kondaron had given him, wondering which spirit might be watching over him, and if the spirit really could protect him. He was tempted to break open the bark to have a look, but he knew that would be the worst thing he could possibly do. In one fell swoop, he would undermine the morale of his companions, upset their beliefs, and turn Kondaron against him for years to come. And perhaps the spirit might get angry and do him harm. No, better follow Kondaron's advice and be cautious. Caution was a virtue that Orinha had begun to learn in his suffering and that he now intended to nurture. His thoughts turned to Kondaron's story. Would he have chosen to eat the human flesh or the bear meat? At first blush, it seemed clear to him that he would have opted for the bear meat, even though he had gone out of his way to become a warrior. What did that mean? On the eve of risking his life in combat, Orinha wondered if he had made the right choice. He would have liked to know for sure.

For his part, Kondaron was relieved to have helped Orinha. At the risk of angering his guardian spirit, he'd taken a small piece of a charred wood from his own bag and cut off the top of the pine tree he had chopped down for that very purpose. Then, he'd placed the talismans in a bark cylinder for Orinha to wear throughout the campaign, for as long as he was Kondaron's responsibility. After the campaign, he would ask

Orinha to give him back the cylinder and help Orinha find his own guardian spirit. Kondaron had devised this solution so that all his warriors could go off to war with the best possible chance of success.

He was confident because his spirit was one of the most powerful. For as long as he could remember, his father and uncles had placed high hopes in him. They often told him he was born under a lucky star. And when the time came for him to leave childhood behind, all his family were convinced the change would do him good and the spirits would continue to support him. But the encounter that would change his life was still far away. After a week spent fasting alone in a small bark shelter, nothing had yet happened. Hunger tormented him, almost to the point of unconsciousness. He even feared he would have to abandon his quest. The spirits seemed to have abandoned him. Without warning, a violent storm erupted. In the small bark shelter swept by the wind and rain, Kondaron was terrorized. Lightning streaked across the sky and thunder reverberated throughout the forest. Suddenly lightning cracked right where Kondaron was looking. Dazzling white-hot light flooded over him for minutes at a time. The trunk of a fir tree shattered and fell, very slowly, heavily toward him, like a giant shadow looming in the blinding light, its top gently brushing past his arm, like a caress...

When the storm was over, Kondaron could see again and realized it had been the encounter he had been hoping for. The spirit of the Thunderbird, one of the most powerful, one of the most formidable, had shown itself with all its might and touched him, transfigured him. The Thunderbird was his guardian spirit. Kondaron then broke off the top of the fir tree and gathered some of the scorched trunk. Back home, he secretly put them in a leather bag he had made, the same bag he wore to this day, the bag that had always brought him luck.

Each time Orinha found sleep, a frightening dream hit him: an enemy cracked his skull open, he fell into a precipice, the Erie devoured him. He woke up with a jump and, eyes wide open, gazed for a moment at the thousands of stars glistening in the infinite sky. The wind rustled the leaves, which stirred in the night. The peace and quiet calmed him a little. But he realized he did not understand the link between the message of peace from the great prophet Deganawida and his father's desire to have them sow terror to the ends of the earth. Why must salvation for all involve the death of so many? There was something in this way of thinking that he could not quite grasp.

Once again sleep overcame him.

In the early hours of the morning, Ganaha awakened him with a violent shake. Orinha was the only one still asleep. All the other warriors were preparing to leave, their faces daubed with war paint, weapons at the ready, impatient and nervous. When he saw the painted face leaning over him, Orinha leaped to his feet, ready to fight for his life. The scene reminded him of the day he was captured. But by then he was awake. He recognized his brother and pulled himself together. There wasn't a minute to lose. Ganaha painted broad strips of brown, black, and red over his face as Orinha swallowed a piece of cold meat. He picked up his musket, his tomahawk, his bow and his arrows, checked that the medicine bag Kondaron gave him was still there, around his waist, and caught up with the others. They ran to the river and flung their canoes into the water.

"I'm going with you!" Orinha shouted after his brother.

"Kondaron knows. We will always fight together. Don't worry."

Orinha, Ganaha, Otasseté, and Shononses teamed up in one of the big canoes. Atotara climbed into the second with Kondaron, Tahira, and Deconissora. Tahonsiwa and Thadodaho took their places in the small canoe. The two young warriors led the war party as it set off toward the Erie fishermen.

CHAPTER 7

ATTACK!

THE MEN PADDLED RESOLUTELY up the stream. It was still in flood and they advanced easily, sometimes carrying their canoes over obstacles or eagerly beating a path along the bank. As soon as they reached the lake where Orinha and Atotara had spotted the Erie fishermen, they hid their canoes in the woods and set out around the lake on foot. At about midday they caught sight of the fishing huts. Kondaron went on ahead to scout around. When he returned, he whispered: "I counted five men and four women gathered around the huts. I don't see anyone on the lake. We'll attack without muskets. Everyone ready." Orinha thought it just as well he persuaded Atotara not to attack using their firearms. He threw his companion an accusing look, which Atotara pretended not to see. Ganaha whispered into his brother's ear: "They don't stand a chance. It's going to be a breeze." Their chief moved ahead and motioned the others to follow him: "On my signal," he whispered, "we all attack at once."

Taking every precaution as they crawled through the high grass, they drew closer to the unsuspecting fishermen closer and closer along the shore. Suddenly Kondaron let out a terrifying cry, stood straight up, and fired an arrow into the closest man. Eight other Iroquois followed suit, roaring at the top of their lungs. A flurry of arrows struck the Erie, as the warriors stormed the helpless fishermen. Orinha was so surprised at how fast everything was moving that he was always a second behind his companions. In an instant, the Iroquois had leaped on their prey like wolves: one struck a runaway down with his tomahawk; the others clubbed anyone who tried to resist. Orinha struck a man that Ganaha had wounded and finished him off. A woman sprawled on the ground was easy pickings for him. The skirmish lasted only a few seconds. No Erie survived.

The ten Iroquois then scalped their victims, proudly holding their prizes up and shouting with joy. As a precaution, Ganaha ran over to the huts to make sure no one was hiding there. Orinha followed him. The first was empty, but an old woman was in the second, paralyzed by fear. Without any hesitation, Ganaha dispatched her with a blow of his club to the head. Orinha, distraught at his brother's violent reflex, could not hold back: "What did you do that for? She wasn't doing anybody any harm!"

"Not so," Ganaha replied calmly. "She could have told the others there were only ten of us and the Erie would have hunted us down. Think about it, Orinha: we're far from home with nobody to help us. There are thousands of Erie here, all around us. There's no mercy: it's them or us. Take her outside; then come with me. There's something else we have to do."

Orinha threw the woman's body, still bleeding, over his shoulders and added it to the pile of mutilated corpses. Ganaha took her scalp and Kondaron handed one to each warrior. All were happy to display the sign of victory on their belts: ten enemies down, without danger or injury! Orinha was not used to revelling in death and felt uncomfortable with a bloody scalp hanging from his belt. The image of his friends' scalps flashed before him. But he forced himself to think like an

Iroquois: every scalp compensated for the death of a warrior fallen in battle. He thought of Orinha, Garagonké's real son, whom he was replacing, whose tragic death he had now made amends for. Now he was fully entitled to bear his name. Orinha said to himself, "So be it: a balance needs to be restored between the spirit world and our world." The thought brought him comfort.

It was time to decide what to do next. Kondaron suggested they find the village where the fishermen were living to carry out a surprise attack before the Erie discovered the massacre and mounted a defence. He wanted to strike like lightning while they still could. Everyone agreed with the strategy. They grabbed any objects of value belonging to the fishermen: charms, pipes, headbands, an old iron knife. Then they threw the bodies into the lake after weighing them down with rocks.

Before Kondaron led the group west, where he believed they would find the enemy village, Ganaha gave Orinha some advice: "Keep your eyes peeled. If Kondaron and I are killed, if we all die apart from you, you must find your way back to the canoes and flee to our village to tell everyone about our victory and how bravely we fought. Keep your wits about you, Orinha. Your life depends on it. And I promise you that if you die and I survive, I will tell our father Garagonké how well you fought."

They covered the distance on the run, in Indian file, bent double so no one could see them. Orinha stayed on Ganaha's heels, registering every landmark ten times more carefully than usual. As the hours went by, in spite of his fatigue, he thought about his attitude, telling himself that the next time they attacked, he would have to react instantaneously, just like his companions. That was what a real Iroquois warrior did: he exploded and showed no mercy. Orinha felt sick at the thought of the poor fishermen they had surprised and massacred just because they were Erie. But he understood: kill or be killed was the iron law. War was without mercy.

They kept running, but slower, so as not to tire themselves out. Silence and vigilance were their watchwords. At the head of the group, Kondaron seemed to know where he was leading his warriors. Ganaha and Orinha were right behind him. Shononses, their best archer, brought up the rear. When evening came, they stopped to regain their strength and eat the fish they took from the fishermen. These they cooked over a tiny fire that they put out as soon as they could lest someone see the smoke. Otasseté and Tahonsiwa took turns standing guard through the night.

In the early hours of the morning, they were awakened by women's voices singing, echoing in the distance. The troop headed toward them right away. After a few minutes' walk, they saw the women hoeing the soil around young corn shoots. Kondaron made a long detour around them. He and his companions soon came within sight of a large Erie village surrounded by a high stockade. They stopped at the edge of the wood, crouched in the undergrowth, weapons in hand. The village was no more than one hundred paces away. This time Kondaron motioned to his warriors to use their muskets to terrorize and kill or wound as many Erie as possible.

Kondaron's plan was to wait until the women returned from the fields before attacking. The women would walk right by them, no doubt accompanied by a few men, and the gate to the village would open to let them in. They would use the confusion sowed by their musket salvo to quickly attack the village and take prisoners, before making their escape.

The plan was a good one, but waiting under the burning sun was easier said than done. They had nothing to drink and hunger gnawed at them. Ganaha could not take it any longer and motioned to Orinha and Shononses beside him that he was going to try to get into the village to get water. "Its sheer madness!" thought Orinha, afraid that his brother wouldn't come back and would spoil their plan. But he could not raise a fuss for fear of drawing attention to the troop. Helpless, he looked on as his brother crept away, walked around the stockade to the back of the village, and disappeared. Orinha despaired! The wait was unbearable. Parched and terrified, he had to make a superhuman effort to stay hidden.

At last, deliriously happy, Orinha saw his brother reappear at the foot of the stockade. He was carrying a huge leather water skin and broke cover to run over to the undergrowth where they were hiding. "He's so brave!" thought Orinha. If there had been sentries posted on top of the stockade, if the Erie had been the least bit suspicious, they would surely have spotted him. Ganaha lay down in the high grass, tired but proud of himself. He crawled over to Orinha and Shononses and gave them a drink. The fresh water invigorated them. Ganaha's daring fired their courage. Ganaha moved from one warrior to another to quench their thirst. When he reached Kondaron, he explained that he found a way into the village through a gap in the stockade. It had been risky, but Kondaron did not dare chide him, since the water was so welcome and everything had worked out so well. His plan remained unchanged, and Ganaha returned to his post beside Orinha, who was now galvanized by his brother's daring. Trembling with excitement, he promised himself he would be just as extraordinary when they next attacked.

The sun was setting on the far horizon when the group of women finally made their way back to the village. Orinha counted eleven women and five men. They were carrying stone tomahawks and long wooden tools for working the soil. Only two men were armed with bows and arrows. Orinha was tense in the extreme as he awaited Kondaron's signal. He could already hear the Erie chatting among themselves and paid close attention to the strange sound of their language, which he had never heard before. The Iroquois chief waited patiently, hoping the guards would fling the gate to the village wide open so they could rush in and fire at all the Erie within range.

But a sharp-eyed woman spotted one of the Iroquois hiding in the bushes. She shouted and pointed at him to sound the alarm. The two archers prepared to fire at Atotara and Tahonsiwa while the rest of the Erie ran for the village. Kondaron knew there was still time to intercept them and answered the woman's cry with a blood-curdling scream of his own, which had all his warriors charging out from their hiding place. Ten shots rang out at once, and two of the Erie collapsed to the ground. The wounded hobbled on as the Iroquois closed in on the enemy, brandishing their knives. Four men stood their ground to fight.

Orinha attacked right away and struck the wounded man nearest him as hard as he could. The Erie could not avoid his club and collapsed in a heap, lifeless. Then, Orinha went after the Erie who were trying to get away, without a thought for the archer behind him, who had him in his sights. Fortunately, Ganaha had his wits about him and leaped on the archer, stabbing him with his knife. Orinha caught up with their fleeing victims just as the guards were hesitantly opening the gate to the village. The young Iroquois warrior didn't even think twice about grabbing one of the women by the hair, tossing her to the ground, then yanking on her locks to get her to run the other way.

Ganaha killed the only man who tried to run away, throwing a tomahawk at his back. He then rushed to help Otasseté, who was having trouble overpowering the second archer to take him prisoner. Tahira stood in the way of a woman and easily captured her, but she bit him and ran away. Tahira caught her and killed her with a blow from his tomahawk. Meanwhile, Kondaron and Shononses seized a man by the waist and were struggling to take him prisoner. But he put up such resistance that they beat him harder still and finally killed him. Kondaron scalped him while Tahonsiwa and Deconissora cut the throats of two injured women who were trying to crawl back to the village. Quickly they scalped them and walked off with their trophy. Ganaha recovered his tomahawk and scalped the dead man. Shononses grabbed hold of a slightly injured woman who was playing dead and dragged her behind him.

Cries were coming from all sides. Nine bodies littered the ground. Only four women had managed to escape. Several Erie archers had now taken positions atop the village stockade, firing arrows down at them. Orinha shoved his prisoner harder to hurry away from the danger. Kondaron shouted for all the warriors to leave—now! Arrows were whistling around them. The chief stood his ground for a moment to make sure all the Iroquois were accounted for, then moved to the head of the troop and fled, bringing two women and a man with them without stopping to collect the scalps of all their victims. Too risky.

The Iroquois ran flat out, dragging or shoving their prisoners, who were also running for their lives. Orinha saw blood everywhere; his ears were still ringing with cries of terror. He kept hold of his prisoner like a living trophy, drunk with victory. Even though their plan had almost come to naught, they were once again victorious and everyone had escaped unscathed. It was true that the spirits were with them. But Tahonsiwa, turning round, saw a hundred warriors pour out of the village and come after them in hot pursuit. They were not out of the woods yet. Faster and faster they ran, to save their skin. As far as they could go they ran, breathless, exhausted. They did not stop until nightfall.

As the moon was almost full and the sky cloudless, they had no difficulty seeing what lay ahead of them. Kondaron decided that he and his companions must go on. They waded down a river to disappear without a trace. Come morning, the two women were exhausted. One was injured, the other livid. They were slowing the troop down too much. Kondaron ordered they be executed, for the safety of the group. Shononses cracked his prisoner's skull open with his tomahawk. But Orinha couldn't bring himself to kill his prisoner in cold blood; she tried so hard to save her life. He asked Ganaha to kill her instead, and felt sick to his stomach when the two bodies were scalped then flung into the river, grim victims of the frantic flight. It was a cold calculation: the lives of the Iroquois against their own, their deaths bereft of glory or defiance, a question of speed, no more, no less. They set off again, moving as fast as they could until evening, lungs on fire, throats red raw, muscles shaking, fear in the pits of their stomachs. The survival instinct of animals.

After a night of rest, the war party made an early start at first light, along with its only remaining prisoner. They headed due south, cutting through the woods. The branches and brushwood scratched their bodies as they went. From time to time, they forced themselves to follow a river or a stream, walking in the water to cover their tracks. The Erie had probably given up the hunt, but how could they be sure? Kondaron did not want to take the risk. He and his warriors would cover as much distance as possible so that their enemies would be afraid to venture too far from home. At any rate, they would have to continue the offensive in another region. Without saying a word, they suffered in silence and followed the tireless Kondaron.

THEY REACHED THE OUTSKIRTS of a region badly damaged by fire. There they found little to eat, and hunger struck quickly. They set up a makeshift camp on a small hill, in the middle of a broad expanse of undergrowth that had started to grow back amidst the charred trees. From there, it would be easy to see the enemy coming. The undamaged forest was no more than an hour's walk away, and the warriors went off in threes and fours to hunt there during the day. But the game seemed to have abandoned the area and, more often than not, they returned empty-handed.

Kondaron wanted the prisoner to tell them where the Erie villages were, where the best hunting was to be had, and more about the region in general. But it seemed he would rather die than reveal anything to the Iroquois, despite the burns they inflicted on his body, despite the two fingers they cut off so he could never hold a bow again. In any event, the man did not understand Iroquois, or Algonquin, and the Iroquois did not understand the Erie language. Only Orinha thought he could make out the odd word. In the hope of getting the prisoner to tell them what he knew, Kondaron ordered that their meagre meal be shared with him. The decision didn't go down well; some members of the party even began to call their chief's authority into question.

Soon, a day of heavy rain made the situation worse. The warriors had nothing with which to protect themselves from the bad weather. It was all they could do to keep their powder dry. Tensions came to a boil the next day, when the Iroquois who'd stayed behind at camp heard three shots ring out in the distance, despite Kondaron's clear instructions to use only bows and arrows. Kondaron, Otasseté, Shononses, and Tahira immediately prepared to defend the camp while Ganaha and Orinha went off to scout the nearby forest. They waited anxiously at its edge, fearing the Erie had ambushed their companions. Then, more shots rang out.

At day's end Ganaha and Orinha were relieved to see that the others had come to no harm. The four hunters returned from the day's expedition with two small partridges, a hare, and plenty of swagger. They had used their muskets despite Kondaron's orders and clearly had no regrets. The situation was becoming intolerable. Before animosity shattered the group, they met to try and work things out.

All the members of the war party gathered together in a circle around a foul-smelling, half-burned fire. The exposed area around them only added to the feeling of destitution that had been weighing on them for days. Night fell. Tahonsiwa spoke for the defiant hunters. They'd made up their minds to use their firearms, he explained, when a deer bounded out of the range of their bows after their best efforts to hit it. They agreed they would have to use their muskets if they wanted to bring anything back. They managed then to bring down two partridges.

"You brought us to this wasteland, where we all might die of hunger," Tahonsiwa continued, "and you won't let us use our muskets! It doesn't make any sense! Are you frightened of the Erie? If you are, you're no longer our chief. Deconissora, Thadodaho, Atotara, and I have had enough. The animals and spirits have all left. We say let's get on with it and attack the Erie. We want more victories."

Tahonsiwa's words were met with uncomfortable silence. The only sound was the crackling of the fire. Their contested chief thought long and hard before he replied.

"You speak well, Tahonsiwa. You are a brave warrior, and you did well to try to kill a deer that would have fed us for days. But you seem to forget that the Erie are many. They know their lands better than we do. We were fortunate enough to claim a second victory without losing a single warrior. But we have had to flee here to escape the vengeance of the enemies who are pursuing us. Until our prisoner can lead us to safety, we must continue to be careful."

"And we've had enough of feeding the prisoner!" Tahonsiwa shot back.

"He must die," added Thadodaho. "He'll tell us nothing."

"You are wrong, Kondaron," Deconissora said. "We must attack the Erie now, not risk this man sounding the alarm. Let's kill him and eat him, not feed him. You need to get back on track and lead us into battle as you promised."

While the men protested, Kondaron fell silent, and attempted to reconcile their opinion with his own. Meanwhile, Ganaha, who was sitting to the right of Kondaron, looked at Orinha, Otasseté, Shononses, and Tahira to see what they thought. He wanted to keep faith with his chief, but felt him bending to maintain his authority and keep the group together. All were hanging on Kondaron's every word.

"So be it. We will execute our prisoner. We will also leave this hostile land, where even the animals no longer want to live. You are right, Tahonsiwa. It would be a bad idea to stay here any longer. But should we attack the Erie now or later? I want to know what each of you thinks. It's your turn to speak."

"Let's attack!" exclaimed young Atotara, without a second's reflection.

"I will follow you, Kondaron," said Shononses. "You are our chief and I am with you."

Orinha glanced at Ganaha out of the corner of his eye, waiting to hear what his older brother thought before he spoke up, because he would rather be on his side, whatever happened, even though he wanted Kondaron to stay on as chief. He did not get on very well with Tahonsiwa, the ringleader of the rebels, who seemed to be the meanest member of the group, perhaps because of the deep scar that ran across his cheek, perhaps because he so rarely smiled. But he was surprised to hear his wise words now that he had gotten much of what he wanted.

"I will follow you into Erie territory until you decide the time is right to attack," declared Tahonsiwa. "I have confidence in the spirits guiding you—if *you* have confidence in them again too! You are my chief and I will follow your advice. But let's not spend another day here. I see that you have understood my point of view and I am thankful for it."

"I think the same as Atotara," said Deconissora. "Let's attack the Erie as soon as we can! There is nothing to be gained by staying here."

"Yes, let's leave now," added Thadodaho. "I am still waiting to kill my first Erie and my tomahawk is growing impatient. I will follow our chief, provided he leads us quickly to the Erie. If not..."

Thadodaho did not finish his sentence, preferring to let the threat hang in the air and add to the pressure already on Kondaron. It was now up to the others to speak. Ganaha looked as though he wanted to hear what Otasseté—the oldest and most level-headed member of the group—and Tahira had to say, before he gave his own opinion. Otasseté understood and spoke up.

"Kondaron has shown wisdom in leading us here," he said calmly. "He has protected us and ensured that each of us still has a chance to claim more victories. He thinks of our brothers, our sisters, and our parents, who want to see all of us come home alive. He has also shown wisdom by listening to Tahonsiwa, who spoke well: it is true that the time has come for us to return to enemy territory. But Kondaron can protect us, he knows how to lead us on to victory, and he is doing what must be done to keep us together. He is our chief and I will follow him to the very end. It is up to him to decide when we attack the Erie again."

"I will do whatever Kondaron decides," added Tahira simply, the more reserved of the two. "Long live our chief! May the spirits be with us!"

Ganaha was the only experienced warrior not to have spoken yet. He saw that Orinha did not want to speak right away.

"My father Garagonké is a war chief respected by all Mohawks," he began. "He is known across the five Iroquois nations for having claimed countless victories against the Susquehannocks, the Mohicans, the Algonquins, the Neutrals, and the Hurons, as well as the French and the Dutch, who fought us unsuccessfully before becoming our allies. He chose Kondaron to lead our war party because, ever since he was born, powerful spirits have guided him and he has already proved he is a great warrior, not to mention a wise and sensible man, despite his young age. Like Otasseté—the oldest among us— said, I support Kondaron and will follow him right to the end. The decision to attack the Erie is his and his alone, when the time and place are right."

Orinha was surprised to see that everyone was now waiting to hear what he had to say, as though his opinion carried as much weight as the experienced warriors who had grown up with war, as though it was up to him to cement or unravel the growing consensus.

"You have all spoken well," he said with humility. "A young warrior like me is keen to absorb everything you say. Like Otasseté and Ganaha, I leave it up to our chief Kondaron. I promise to serve him faithfully and to help each and every one of you to the best of my ability."

Ganaha and the other warriors were pleased at Orinha's attitude. He had understood his place in the group. Everyone was happy to see him learning quickly and maturing well. Kondaron had managed to re-establish his authority by accepting a quick return to Erie territory and agreeing to look for better places to hunt. Nevertheless, he remained serious and modest. He gathered his thoughts in silence, throwing a few handfuls of tobacco on the fire, as was his wont. Then he brought the meeting to a close:

"Let us thank the spirits for casting light on our discussion. Let us thank them for having kept our unity intact. It is our most valuable asset, if our expedition is to succeed. I thank Tahonsiwa for reminding me of my promises and steering me back on course. Tomorrow, we will return to Erie territory in search of a mighty victory. However, I ask each of you to be patient and to wait for a favourable occasion. We must avoid the fury of the Erie: they are courageous warriors and they vastly outnumber us. If we do this, we will all see our families again and they will be proud of us."

A few hours later, Thadodaho took care of executing the prisoner, who was then roasted and eaten. In spite of his hunger and his willingness to imitate his companions in every respect, Radisson struggled to swallow the mouthfuls of human flesh. The meat rolled around his mouth like a foreign body, a poison that he had to force himself not to spit out. Even with his eyes discreetly closed to lessen his disgust, he found this particular Iroquois custom hard to bear. In his distress, images of his past life in Paris and Trois-Rivières briefly resurfaced. Now that his new life had brought him adventure, challenges, friends, and satisfaction in abundance, those images seemed strange and no longer moved him.

THE WIND CHANGES

WEEKS PASSED. After several days of cautious wandering, the Iroquois returned to the first encampment they'd built earlier, near the river. They felt safe there, for the Erie must surely have believed that they'd left the area for good. They were happy to find the powder and provisions they had stored, buried in bark containers. They also recovered the canoes they had hidden near the shore of the small fishing lake. Now they would be able to move around more easily.

Since they had left the barren region that put their unity to the test, they passed through any number of places that teemed with game. They wanted for nothing. But they still had not found the enemy they were looking for. Occasionally they would spot well-armed groups of three and four Erie, out hunting or moving goods. They also discovered a second fortified village, even bigger than the first, which must have been home to at least two thousand people, perhaps more. But Kondaron, supported by the group's leaders, Tahonsiwa, Ganaha, and Otasseté, decided not to attack targets that were too big or too small, so as not to leave themselves open to new reprisals from the Erie.

To avoid being found out, they kept to the borders of the Erie lands, constantly on the move, always in Indian file. They never spent more than two or three days in the same place and used their canoes only at night. And so they encountered fewer enemies. Since they had already killed twenty-two Erie and each boasted at least one scalp hanging from his belt, they preferred to keep the risk to a minimum and wait until the time was right for another great victory. Nevertheless, this strategy too was starting to put their patience to the test.

At last, a chance to ambush and kill the Erie presented itself. They spotted a group of thirty or so Erie far in the distance and tracked them for a whole day. By their estimate, the group numbered as many men as women. They were carrying goods in huge wicker baskets and seemed to be walking to a trading place, perhaps an Erie village, perhaps a village of another nation. Even though they were armed, they were clearly not on the warpath. The Iroquois now knew the region well enough to be certain that no Erie village or camp was less than a day away by foot. Their prey would be far from help. All the conditions for an Iroquois attack were falling into place. Under cover of darkness, Kondaron gave the order to move in.

In the morning, they saw that the group consisted of exactly twenty-one men and twelve women. From a distance, their long hair and identical leather clothing had led the Iroquois to first believe that women were carrying all the baskets, but such was not the case. Three scouts had already taken the lead when the group broke camp. Ten armed men guarded the twenty carriers, five in front and five behind the main group. Unless they were concerned about an Iroquois attack, such precautions indicated that the baskets contained valuables. Kondaron and his troop followed along a short distance behind them, to their right.

The chief kept Ganaha, Otasseté, and Tahonsiwa at his side to advise him. He motioned for them to come closer: "They seem tougher than we thought," he whispered. "Do you still think we should attack?" All three nodded. "Then we have to surround them." He pointed to Otasseté and Tahonsiwa. "You two take the left flank with Tahira, Deconissora, and Thadodaho. I'll stay with Ganaha and the others on this side. We'll surround them completely, on all sides, both front and rear. Our attack will throw them into a panic. Otasseté, when you are all ready, hoot three times like an owl. Then, attack on my signal." Kondaron pointed to his musket and motioned that they would each fire twice from hiding before closing in to fight hand-to-hand. "I'll fire first," added Kondaron. Then, each of you will fire in turn. Our weapons will terrorize them. Let's hope a few of them fall before we move in. All right, let's go!"

Kondaron sent Shononses up to the front on his flank. Atotara went between the two. Kondaron stayed in the centre, with Orinha and Ganaha taking up the rear. But it was much too risky for the other five warriors to outflank the Erie, then take up their positions all the way along the left flank. Those who had to move up front quickened their step. Alas, the man-oeuvre drew the attention of an Erie guard, who caught a glimpse of Tahonsiwa running between the trees. He sounded the alarm immediately. The Erie stopped, closed ranks, and the carriers set down their baskets while the archers got ready to fire at the only enemy they'd seen. But Tahonsiwa hid behind a tree. The tension was thick enough to cut.

Otasseté hooted three times like an owl and Kondaron ordered the attack. He stood up from behind the ferns and real-ized that the Erie were watching their other flank. He took time to aim, then fired and crouched back down in the grass to reload. Nine other shots sounded, one after the other. The Erie did not know which way to turn. The women began to scream. Orinha was already scrambling back to his feet to fire a second round. He drew a bead on an archer whose back was turned, fired, and watched the archer fall face down to the ground. Orinha hid behind his tree again, rushing to reload his musket to fire a third time before Kondaron's signal. More shots rang out. Orinha could hear the Erie shouting and moaning, distraught.

When Kondaron got up to fire a second time, he saw that the Erie had regrouped. They'd formed a circle, protecting themselves behind their baskets. He could see bodies and a few wounded Erie writhing on the ground, but their strategy was paying off. From his hiding place, Kondaron counted the shots apprehensively, waiting for the twentieth before he roared for his men to attack. But before he had finished counting, Atotara stood up next to him, opened fire, and launched the attack. The Erie let fly with a volley of arrows at their one and only target, and the young warrior paid for his daring with his life. Two men pounced on him and finished him off with a stone tomahawk. Shononses seized the opportunity to dash out from his hiding place and fire an arrow at one of them from point-blank range. Orinha fired his third shot at the group of carriers. Still more shots rang out.

Kondaron let out his death yell and leaped from his hiding place at the same time as the eight other demons, letting fly with arrows and brandishing their muskets. The Erie were totally confused. Ganaha planted his tomahawk right in the heart of the man closest to him, who collapsed. The Erie replied as best they could, firing back with arrows, but hand-to-hand fighting had already begun. The Erie's wooden clubs and stone tomahawks banged noisily against the Iroquois' iron weapons. Cries and moans echoed through the forest as both sides lashed out, shoved, dodged, squirmed free, grabbed hold of each other. Enraged, they charged one another, lost hope and retreated. A handful of Erie braves fought on doggedly as others picked up their baskets, administered help to one of the wounded, and fled. None of the Iroquois gave chase. Four Erie kept up the fight and counterattacked the Iroquois with ferocity. When the last Erie had been beaten to the ground, Kondaron ordered his men to stay where they were, to avoid any ambush the survivors might have prepared. The bitter confrontation had left them all exhausted. A number of Iroquois were injured.

The Erie had shown astonishing courage and energy, despite being surrounded by the Iroquois with their superior weapons. A good twenty of them had survived the attack and managed to escape. Fifteen or so remained on the battlefield, killed or wounded. The Iroquois, breathless and wild-eyed, counted themselves fortunate to have come away with the victory.

Atotara had taken three arrows full in the chest and a tomahawk-blow to the head. He was still breathing weakly, but had no chance of surviving. A tomahawk had shattered Shononses's right arm; he groaned in pain. Tahira snapped off the arrowhead that had pierced his thigh and bravely pulled out the rest of the shaft, grimacing with pain. Deconissora was trying to stop the bleeding after an Erie warrior's stone tomahawk had left him with a gaping chest wound. Orinha and the others had only cuts and bruises. Without the muskets that had sowed such terror and injured so many of their enemies at the start of the battle, they would never have bested the Erie.

With a tomahawk, Tahonsiwa finished off an enemy prisoner left to die among the nine bodies piled up on the ground. Three other Erie, less seriously wounded, were taken captive. The Iroquois took the ten scalps from their latest victims and gathered the spoils left behind by their fleeing enemies: five baskets of cornmeal, bows and arrows, beautifully sculpted clubs, stone pipes, tobacco, deerskins, and goat hair necklaces. Before leaving the danger behind, they lit a huge bonfire and threw Atotara's body onto it, an honour reserved for warriors who died in combat. Then, they took refuge deep in the woods, far from the battlefield, to tend to their wounds and keep the rest of the war party safe.

That night, for all his fatigue, Kondaron stayed awake for a long time to consult the spirits. He made repeated incantations and offerings of sacred herbs: he could sense their anger. When morning came, he did not feel as though he had managed to appease them, or learn more about their uncertain humour. But it would be foolhardy to continue the campaign now, he was sure of it. He held a meeting to share his concerns and hear what the other warriors thought.

"We have claimed three great victories," he explained. "We have taken twenty-five scalps and three prisoners, along with a valuable haul. But I feel that the spirits are no longer with us. We have already lost Atotara and, if we continue to fight, I fear the spirits will abandon us completely. I think it is time to go back home, as soon as the wounded are up to the journey. We will return victorious, our heads held high. Are any of you against ending our offensive?"

"Ho!" shouted Tahira right away, to show his agreement with Kondaron's decision.

The others thought for a moment.

"I agree," spoke Ganaha. "Several of us could have died by Atotara's side. The battle was fierce. Until now, the spirits have been favourable to us. But you are right: if you feel they are abandoning us, we must show them consideration and return to our families to celebrate our victories with them."

"Ho!" added Orinha simply, happy that Kondaron and Ganaha suggested what he had secretly been hoping for since the bitter battle the day before.

Shononses also agreed.

"My wounds are very painful," he said. "I may not be able to paddle, and I certainly cannot fight either, or even hunt. We are vulnerable, Kondaron. You are making the right decision. It is time for us to return home."

Tahonsiwa, Thadodaho, and Deconissora glanced at one another. Deconissora was suffering from his wounds, still bleeding, despite the plaster of medicinal plants the warriors had applied to his chest. He felt very weak, and feared for his life. Waiting for his wounds to heal would slow the group down, but he was eager to leave the land of the Erie. His two companions knew it and supported him.

"Ho!" they said in unison.

"Kondaron is wise," Tahonsiwa added. "He is right. We will leave as soon as we can."

Otasseté kept his silence for a moment, before noting that the time was right to return home.

"The summer is drawing to an end," he said. "If we do not return home as soon as the wounded have recovered, winter might well surprise us along the way, for the journey will be long. We must prepare to leave right away. Which route do you think we should take, Kondaron?"

The chief was pleased to see his warriors agree with his suggestion and that they were happy, too, with all they had accomplished.

"Last year," he replied, "we returned over the mountains. The going is steep, but safe. No enemy lives in these lands, but there is beaver, fish, and game in abundance. Our canoes are hidden nearby and, once we have recovered and repaired them, we will be able to head south, then east through the mountains. The whole time, we will be moving further and further away from the Erie. But if we go back the way we came, we will have to cut across the land of the Erie, or take a long detour around it. That would be dangerous. I suggest we return through the mountains. Our prisoners will help us carry the canoes and our packs. Does everyone agree?"

"Ho! Ho!" the warriors responded as one.

||||||||||||||||||||||||||||||||||||||||||||||||||||||||||||||||||||||||||||||||||||||||||||||||||||||

CHAPTER 9

THE WARRIOR'S RETURN

PREPARATIONS FOR THE JOURNEY took time: the injured recovered slowly and provisions had to be gathered with utmost caution. Once they were a few days out of enemy territory, a feeling of sheer relief swept over Orinha. Even though peace was less exciting than war, he was glad life had returned to normal. Danger was no longer routine. They were no longer in peril, and no longer had to hide all the time. There were no enemies to be tracked down or killed. Life went on peacefully enough, and that was just fine.

At first, the mountains were hard to climb, but soon the warriors and their captives reached a plateau, where stretches of river flowed between lakes that teemed with fish. It was just as well, since their fragile canoes were filled to capacity. The portages were not too frequent, not too hard, and the prisoners carried the heaviest loads. The cornmeal they took from the Erie came in handy. There was no shortage of fresh or smoked fish, or of fresh venison. Life was good and generous.

However difficult the route, Orinha had no trouble staying at the head of the group alongside Ganaha and Kondaron. How he had progressed over the five moons of their journey! He felt proud and confident in his abilities.

The wounded had now recovered. Deconissora had regained some of his aplomb and Shononses no longer grimaced with pain, even though neither of them was as yet up to paddling. Tahira limped a little, but lost none of his stamina.

The nine Iroquois and their three Erie prisoners reached another mountain range. They hauled their canoes up steep slopes, then down to the bottom of roaring waterfalls. Making their way along rocky paths, they carried their packs for long stretches at a time. The Iroquois kept close watch over their prisoners, who were tempted to try to escape, since they were being worked so hard. Shononses and Deconissora still had not forgiven the Erie who wounded them and told them in no uncertain terms that they would kill them if they attempted to get away. But Kondaron gave them all the food they wanted, to provide them with sustenance and encouragement.

The group at last reached familiar territory, where the Iroquois had imposed their law and sometimes came to hunt. Apart from members of their nation, no one came to the area, which abounded with beaver and game of every kind. After locating the spot where last year's war party had set up camp, Kondaron suggested they stay there for a few days to stock up on beaver pelts. They would be returning to the village at the height of the trading season with the Dutch, so the suggestion was welcome.

Over the following days, while Shononses and Deconissora stood guard over the three prisoners tied up at camp, the rest of the Iroquois fanned out to hunt in groups of two and three. Orinha always teamed up with Ganaha. One day, they heard two shots one after the other, followed by a far-off cry for help. Then, they spotted smoke signals. They hurried off in the direction of the smoke and soon found Tahonsiwa.

"Thadodaho and I saw two women. They ran away as soon as they saw us," he told them. "Thadodaho chased after them, but the forest is thick and they managed to hide. We need help finding them."

"We'll help you look for them," Ganaha replied.

Tahonsiwa again roared at the top of his voice, a rallying cry to other warriors who might have been nearby. Ganaha fired another shot into the air. Minutes later, Otasseté and Tahira joined them.

"Let's go to the spot where Thadodaho and the two women disappeared," suggested Tahonsiwa. "We must capture them. Everyone, keep in sight. We'll search every bush, under every tree. They can't have gotten far."

"Let's find Thadodaho first. He'll be able to point us in the right direction," said Ganaha. "We won't let them get away."

They quickly found their companion, waiting for help on the shore of a small bay.

"They can't have crossed the lake," said Thadodaho. "I was watching carefully. The last time I saw them, they ran off that way."

The search was swift and efficient. Ganaha and Tahonsiwa needed only a few minutes to find the two women squatting helplessly at the foot of a tall fir tree. Exhausted, famished, and resigned, they did not attempt to run away. The six Iroquois took them straight back to camp where, shy and frightened, they devoured everything put in front of them. They spoke a language similar to Algonquin, which Orinha and Otasseté had no problem making out. The two warriors were promptly put in charge of interrogating the two women.

"Which nation are you from? Where are you from?" they asked.

"The Mississauga nation," one of them replied.

The other woman remained silent.

"Where are you from? Answer me!" Otasseté asked the other, brandishing his club.

"Don't hit us!" the first woman answered, covering her head with both hands.

"Are you lost?" asked Orinha. "Nobody lives here. Only the Iroquois hunt here."

"Yes," replies the same woman. "We're lost. Help us. Please don't hurt us."

Unsure of how to react, Orinha and Otasseté glanced at each other. The second woman still hadn't said a word. Despite her haggard looks, her sunken cheeks, and the feverish look in her eyes, there was no denying her beauty. Orinha immediately took pity on her.

"They must be escaped prisoners," Kondaron concluded. He had been listening to the exchange and made out a few words. "The Mississaugas have been on the run ever since we defeated the Hurons. Ask them who captured them."

"Who captured you?" Otasseté asked in Algonquin. "When did you escape? Answer me! Or your scalps will be hanging over my fireplace!"

The two women looked despairingly at each other. The woman who had not yet spoken at last opened her mouth.

"Tell them!" she said to her companion, without looking up at her captors.

"The Iroquois captured us with twenty other Mississaugas and Hurons," the more talkative of the two said, hesitantly and fearfully. "We returned to hunt on our land, thinking the Iroquois had left for good. But they were still here. They were waiting for us. They killed many of our men in an ambush, then captured us and brought us to their lands."

"Iroquois from which nation?" Kondaron asked Otasseté, who repeated the question in Algonquin.

"I don't know," she replied. "They were cruel Iroquois," she added, lowering her eyes.

"Go on!" Otasseté orders. "When did you escape?"

Staring at the ground, the woman continued her story. Her voice was barely audible.

"There were twelve warriors. They watched the men especially. One night, Maniska and I ran away into the woods. That was five days ago."

"And we got lost," Maniska, the good-looking one, added. "We don't know where we are. We are too far from our land." Then, she broke into sobs.

"She is lucky we recaptured them," thought Orinha. "Otherwise, they would have starved."

Kondaron ordered his warriors to tie them up and bring them to wait with the other prisoners, while they decided what to do with them. Otasseté took the talkative one, and Orinha took Maniska. Orinha was struck by how delicate she was, how brave, how fragile. As he gently tied her hands behind her back, he could not help whispering to her, in Algonquin: "You're safe now. Don't worry." Her fate was not in his hands, but that did not stop him imagining ways to spare her life...

The capture of the women changed the course of the war party. That evening, Kondaron held a meeting. The eight warriors gathered in a circle around the fire to listen to what their chief had to say.

"There are now fourteen of us, and we already have furs to carry too," he explained. "Our canoes are no longer enough. We will have to build at least one more. I suggest we build two, to spread the load and make sure we return home safely. We will take the time we need to build the canoes, and to hunt beaver and other animals. It is late in the year and people in the village will be even happier to see us if we return with plenty of provisions. The two women will help us prepare the pelts. I suggest we spend two more weeks here. We will hunt as much as we can, while Otasseté, Shononses, and Tahira build the canoes."

A brief moment of reflection was all that was needed to win the approval of all. Starting the next morning, Orinha started trapping beaver with unbridled enthusiasm. His eagerness surprised even Ganaha, who knew him well. Since beavers were few and far between in the Iroquois lands, Ganaha instructed his younger brother to lower his sights, forbidding him to kill mothers and young, just as their forefathers used to do. To please the older brother he admired so much, Orinha agreed to curb the fever for trade that had taken hold of him and spare the lives of the few additional beavers that he would have trapped before Ganaha spoke to him. Every evening when he came back from the hunt, Orinha brought fish and roast meat to Maniska. He made sure, too, that she was treated well during the day. Shononses quickly noticed Orinha's interest in the prisoner and, to please his young companion and friend, now watched over Maniska like a father. Orinha tried to make it look as though he was looking after the other prisoner with just as much care, in case it appeared that he was enamoured of the prettiest and jealousy were to raise its head. Shononses wasn't fooled for a second, but had no objections. Tahonsiwa, on the other hand, didn't like the adopted Frenchman hovering around his prisoners. He reckoned they belonged to him: after all, he saw them first. And so Tahonsiwa kept a discreet eye on his spoils. Meanwhile Thadodaho and Ganaha had claims of their own, since they had helped capture them. Seeing that Tahonsiwa was trying to keep them away from the prisoners, they complained to Kondaron, who was responsible for dividing up the spoils of the war party before they returned to the village. Each warrior wanted to gain as much merit as possible from his victories, and bring back his fair share of trophies for his family. Their chief would decide.

For the moment, all were grateful for the goodwill shown by the two prisoners, who made leather pouches for storing bear and deer fat. They also busied themselves preparing the beaver pelts and making meals for the three Erie prisoners. They were proving very useful. Orinha for one was sure they were worth more to them alive than dead. He had even given up on his original idea and now hoped to give Maniska to his mother as a slave to help her with her many chores around the house. It would be only fair after all that Katari had done for him—not to mention that she would be living in the same longhouse as him, at his side.

THE NEW CANOES were ready; hunting had brought its rewards. The time had come to return to the village. Ganaha and Orinha loaded up their new canoe with three big bundles of beaver pelts and a leather pouch full of bear fat. Over Tahonsiwa's protests, Maniska climbed in with them, leaving Tahonsiwa to make the return journey with Thadodaho and the other prisoner. His canoe was also laden with pelts and part of the spoils taken from the Erie. Kondaron decided to travel with the youngest Erie prisoner, who had shown good-will and was trying hard to learn the basics of the Iroquois language. The chief promised to spare his life if he proved himself worthy of his trust. The Erie sat in the bow where Kondaron could keep an eye on him. Their load consisted of two packs of smoke-cured meat.

The other two prisoners, either too stubborn or too percep-tive to try to curry favour with the Iroquois, would doubtless be tortured and put to death as soon as they reached the vil-lage. In the eyes of Tahira, Shononses, and Deconissora, who guarded them closely, they were the most precious spoils from the whole campaign since they would be used to avenge the injuries the Erie had inflicted on them. They would also have to leave one of them with the Oneida to compensate for the death of young Atotara. Shononses and Otasseté took one of these prisoners with them in their canoe, along with pelts and a pouch of moose fat. Deconissora and Tahira took the third prisoner, as well as a pack of pelts and some smoke-cured meat.

After the two marvellous weeks spent hunting, piling up beaver pelts, bear fat, and smoked meat, Orinha savoured every moment of the smooth trip home. He rediscovered the fascinating charms of womenfolk, as he admired Maniska travelling ahead of him, strong and sturdy for all her small and graceful body. She paddled with precision, steadily and skilfully, and it was clear that she was used to getting around in a canoe. Orinha admired her every movement, each more harmonious than those of his companions. At the same time, he delighted in the play of the autumn light as it sparkled on the landscape around them, dancing off the crystal-clear water in a thousand reflections and setting the leaves of the forest ablaze with colour. He breathed in the fresh air, paddled, ate, laughed, and gazed at Maniska for hours on end. Each gift of life seemed absolutely priceless and full of goodness to him.

Before they reached the Mohawk River that would carry them home, Kondaron gave the order to make an important stop. They had already encountered friends and family from neighbouring villages, and news of their arrival would spread quickly. It was time to share the spoils, before the cheering and praise went to their heads. They beached their canoes on a sandy tongue of land and bound all five prisoners tightly, hand and foot, including the two women and the young Erie whose life Kondaron had promised to spare. For the last time as chief of the campaign, Kondaron stood to address his warriors, who were gathered in a circle.

"Here we are at the end of our adventure," he said solemnly. "With the exception of Atotara, we must thank the spirits for bringing us all back safe and sound after our long and danger-ous journey. Let us thank them for granting us three victories and allowing us to bring so many scalps and prisoners back to our families. The spirits were truly on our side. You also conducted yourselves with great bravery. You fought with cun-ning and determination—and you won."

Listening as Kondaron looked back on their journey, Orinha saw a stream of surprising images pass through his mind. He recalled the first difficult days of walking, the wonderful cross-ing of the great lake, and the fear he had felt as they entered enemy territory. He could still see their first attack clearly: his dithering and confusion, the failed ambush at the gates to the Erie village, and their frantic getaway. His body could still feel the blows from the last, bitter battle. He thought of his com-panions' wounds, of Atotara's death. So much had happened in so little time! He felt as though he had undergone a pro-found transformation. He was now a seasoned warrior.

All around him, everyone seemed lost in thought. No one broke the long silence imposed by Kondaron; all waited for their chief to continue with his speech.

"It has been a long time since a party of nine warriors returned home with so many scalps and prisoners, with so many spoils taken from the enemy, with so many beaver pelts, so much meat and fat. You are all deserving of your share of the spoils. You all deserve the glory that will be showered upon us when our families, our clans, and everyone in the village hail our return and welcome us as heroes. But first, I would like the prisoners we left behind and the scalps we couldn't bring back with us to be counted as part of the spoils. Orinha, the youngest among us, fought like a man and deserves our admiration. Ganaha always supported me. Otasseté, the most experienced of us all, was always there to advise me. Tahonsiwa put me back on the right path. Shononses, Deconissora,

Tahira, and Thadodaho, my brothers, let us celebrate together and share in our spoils."

Kondaron had laid out all the scalps at his feet before beginning his speech. Solemnly, he handed out two scalps to each warrior, keeping none for himself and leaving nine on the ground as though they belonged to no one. Next came the delicate matter of dividing up the prisoners. In a loud voice, Kondaron continued:

"Tahira and Shononses, you will see to it that no one mistreats the tallest and the strongest of our prisoners when we return to the village. In the days to come, you will lead him to the Oneida and present him to Atotara's family. This prisoner will make up for the death of the youngest warrior among us. To each of you, I give an additional scalp for your injuries."

For the first time, a handful of warriors showed signs of discontent. Orinha saw it clearly.

"The youngest Erie prisoner is mine," Kondaron goes on. "I promised him I would spare his life and I will watch over him. My clan will adopt him. This prisoner is enough for me. I do not want a scalp, or any of the things we took from the Erie. You will share them among yourselves. Having been your chief gives me as much satisfaction as these precious spoils. Deconissora nearly died at the hands of the enemy and deserves the other Erie prisoner. Deconissora, do with him what you will."

Sensing the growing impatience of a few of the warriors, Orinha saw that the solidarity that had united them thus far would not last. In particular, he noticed the tense expressions on the faces of Tahonsiwa, Thadodaho, and Tahira. Their pursed lips were doing all they could to hold back floods of protest. Kondaron must have seen it coming, but the inexperienced Orinha was caught unawares. He too was now on edge, ready to react, glancing at Ganaha, who remained perfectly expressionless. Kondaron continued his efforts to resolve the sensitive issue of the prisoners.

"The two women will be shared between—"

"The two women belong to me!" Tahonsiwa cried out angrily.

"No they don't!" retorted Orinha, cut to the quick. "That's not true, Tahonsiwa! They're not yours!"

"And why would they belong to you?" asked Ganaha, who saw the whole thing coming. "Didn't you call us to help you find and capture them? Didn't I see them at the same time as you?"

"Don't forget I followed them through the forest," Thadodaho broke in. "Without me, we would never have found them again! One of them belongs to me!"

Kondaron tried to calm everyone with his body language. Everyone wanted a share of the prisoners, the most precious of their spoils, but there were only five prisoners for nine warriors.

"My brothers," Kondaron said firmly, "the women must be shared, because none of you deserves to have both."

"I was the one who found them," insisted Tahonsiwa. "I led the search."

"You are forgetting the two women we killed when we were fleeing the Erie village," replied Orinha. "Shononses and I captured them."

"Shononses already has a prisoner and you both have one of their scalps," Tahonsiwa replied, not in the least impressed.

"He's not my prisoner," retorted Shononses. "Tahira and I are going to give him to Atotara's family, who will decide what to do with him. He's not my prisoner, or Tahira's. He belongs to Atotara's family."

"Tahonsiwa is behaving like a child," said Otasseté firmly, trying to bring the quarrel to an end. "He claims to be wise and to know what is best for us all, but he's only thinking of himself. Tahonsiwa should be quiet and listen to Kondaron. Perhaps Thadodaho is right, perhaps he does deserve the women more than you. Listen to your chief and learn from his wisdom."

Tahonsiwa swallowed his anger and held his tongue. The tension dropped a notch. Orinha had thought that taking Maniska in their canoe had meant she belonged to him and his brother. But he could see it was far from a foregone conclusion. He didn't care what Tahonsiwa wanted: he was prepared to fight for Maniska's life. He knew that Ganaha was thinking the same thing he was thinking: they both wanted to give her to Katari. Tahonsiwa, on the other hand, wanted to kill the two women. Ganaha stood up to lend extra weight to his opinion and broke the tense silence.

"Orinha and I are from the same family," he said. "We want to give Maniska to our mother as a slave. Katari is not as young as she used to be and she needs a helping hand. She deserves this woman, and we do too—we fought as well as any man here. Orinha also captured a prisoner we weren't able to bring with us and I killed her with my own hands. Between the two of us, we certainly deserve Maniska. If anyone challenges our will, let him stand."

Nobody moved, or replied to Ganaha, not even Kondaron, who simply nodded his agreement. Satisfied, Ganaha sat back down. Kondaron continued to divide up the spoils.

"There remains one prisoner and seven scalps," he said. "I would like to give the second woman to Tahonsiwa. I hope she will satisfy his greed and calm the resentment he has shown toward his brothers. It is true that Tahonsiwa is a courageous warrior and his advice has been useful to us: he deserves this prisoner. But no more. I will give two more scalps to those who do not have a prisoner. The honour of having killed more enemies than the others will shine down upon them. Otasseté and Thadodaho, take these symbols of strength and courage—they belong to you. The three other scalps will be given to whomever I choose."

Slowly, Kondaron moved from warrior to warrior, looking at each of them closely. Peace had almost returned to the group. Everyone knew their victory was a great one and their return to the village would be triumphant. Each would enjoy every moment of it, especially since Kondaron acted fairly and humbly by keeping the smallest share of the spoils for himself, as any chief worthy of his rank must do. He stopped in front of Thadodaho and handed him another scalp.

"Take this," he told him. "You deserve this scalp for helping capture the women. May the spirits watch over you."

He then stopped before Otasseté.

"Your words often kept us on the right path," he said, "and you are getting older. There will be fewer battles for you. This scalp is just reward for all you did for us."

Finally, Kondaron stopped in front of Orinha, who was bursting with joy after snatching Maniska from the hands of Tahonsiwa. Kondaron put a hand on his shoulder and, in a voice loud enough for everyone to hear, said:

"The final scalp is for you, young Orinha. You brought honour upon your father Garagonké, a great warrior and a great chief. You also brought honour upon Garagonké's oldest son, Orinha, who gave you his name. I knew him well, and you proved yourself his equal. You are now a true Mohawk. Take pride in all you have accomplished."

Then, Kondaron muttered under his breath, so that only Radisson heard him:

"The spirit that guides me has protected you until now. But when we return to the village, you must give me back the bark cylinder I lent you. My spirit can do no more for you. Now, you must follow your own path, and find the spirit that will guide you."

Orinha was a little surprised at the significance Kondaron gave the bark cylinder, but mostly he felt relieved. Even though everything went well, he never really believed that the spirit was helping him. In fact, the bark cylinder he wore around his waist sometimes worried him more than anything else. He feared he might unintentionally discover its secret and anger Kondaron, or the spirit, rather than enjoy its protection. Whatever the case, his life as an Iroquois was now shaping up to be easier and he no longer needed it.

After dividing up the objects taken from the Erie, as well as the food supplies and the beaver pelts, Kondaron again asked his warriors for their attention. Did they agree with how the spoils had been shared? All agreed without further discussion.

Two days later, the warriors reached the trail that led to their village. A small crowd had already gathered on the river-bank with presents and food to celebrate the war party's victorious return. Orinha's favourite sister, Conharassan, was among them. She stood there attentively, well away from the shore, until Orinha waved her forward. Then she ran and jumped into his arms, almost knocking him over. Her eyes full of joy and admiration, Conharassan kissed him passionately. She then kissed Ganaha, like a brother, before coming back to snuggle in Orinha's arms. She took him by the arm, the hand, the waist; she hung from his neck and cast her loving gaze back at his own.

Surprised and delighted by his sister's behaviour, Orinha tore himself away from her to help Ganaha unload the canoe.

Then, he asked her to stand back for a moment as he searched for his gift for her. Both excited and impatient, hands behind her, Conharassan agreed to back up while he searched for her gift. "Here you are," Orinha told her, "Make yourself a nice dress from these two deerskins." Delighted, she kissed her brother again, and then unrolled the animal skins to admire how fine they were, touched and grateful that he had thought of her. Maniska, who had meticulously prepared the deerskins, unloaded the canoe, keeping her eyes on the ground. Orinha was completely captivated by his sister's attentions. She was more beautiful, more mature, and more confident than before. His success as a warrior seemed to have fanned the flames of her affection. For a moment, he forgot his fair prisoner, who felt more threatened than ever in the midst of so many Iroquois.

Messengers ran on ahead to the village to let everyone know how many scalps and prisoners Kondaron and his warriors had brought back from their profitable campaign. Once the canoes had been emptied and hauled far up onto the river-bank, the warriors prepared a feast with the meat and corn their friends and family had given them. They sang and danced with the young women and men come to celebrate their victories. They ate, told tales of their adventures, and rested as they waited for the slaves who would carry their packs to the village the next day. In the meantime, the five prisoners remained bound to stakes beaten into the ground. It would be a calamity if one of them were to escape now, just hours from the great honour of bringing them home.

Conharassan was so happy that Orinha had returned, so proud of the scalps he had brought back, so pleased with the prisoner he wanted to give to Katari, so impressed with all the beaver pelts he would be able to trade with the Dutch, that she spent a passionate night by his side. For his part, he found her so gentle, so warm and sensual, that he was staggered by the love she still felt for him after so long apart. After the dangers and hardships of battle, how wonderful it felt to make love again! All the other warriors spent the night with the women who had been awaiting them, whether a lover or the mother of their children. Ganaha had an emotional reunion with Oreanoué, a young woman from the Wolf clan he was already in love with before he left.

Very early the next morning, an elder from the village arrived at the head of around thirty valorous warriors and twenty-odd clan mothers. They came to acclaim the return of Kondaron and the members of his war party and broke into shouts of joy when they saw that rumours of a great victory were true. They spent a good few minutes congratulating, thanking, and praising the warriors and the spirits. The five prisoners were then untied to help slaves from the village carry part of the load. Apart from the odd tomahawk or knife, neither Kondaron nor his warriors had anything to carry at all.

At each stop, Conharassan greased and combed Orinha's hair. She fed him, fussed over him, and showered him with compliments. Ganaha's beloved Oreanoué treated him equally well.

Before they reached the village, Kondaron made certain that the chief and the thirty warriors who came out to meet them understood his decision: Maniska, the tallest prisoner, and the youngest Erie would all be spared. Messengers were sent ahead to announce the arrangements and defuse tensions, lest frustration in the village boil over. The three would escape the customary beating and be led under guard directly to the longhouses of the Tortoise and Bear clans.

Now the stockade was in sight! Orinha could hear the villagers gathered outside the main gate shouting with joy, stamping their feet with impatience, feverishly waving their arms and brandishing their weapons. A feeling of immense satisfaction swept over him. One year earlier, the same villagers were waiting for him, baying for his blood, ready to beat him until he bled and make him pay for his crimes. They were all against him, everyone except for his dear parents!

These same villagers now welcomed him back as a hero. They praised his victories and cheered his courage. Orinha felt as though he was about to burst from too much happiness and pride. He had managed to reverse what had seemed liked a hopeless situation. Now, his war chief was congratulating him, his sister thought the world of him, his older brother was unreservedly behind him, and his brothers in arms respected him. Better still, it was he who would decide whether Maniska lived or died. He could give her the most precious thing ever given to him: the gift of life, just like a god or a spirit. How proud he was!

To the clamour of the villagers, the troop neared the stockade. The nine warriors had taken the lead, and came to a stop before the chief who had come out to meet them: the spoils of victory belonged to them and them alone. Their hour of glory had come. On the final steps of their journey, they strutted about as modestly as they could manage, holding or carrying their twenty-five scalps or displaying them at the end of a pole, their five prisoners tied to them on a leash. Orinha's happiness knew no bounds when he saw his mother emerge from the crowd and walk straight up to him and Ganaha. Katari sang and leaped with joy as she saw her two sons home at last, hale, hearty, and victorious. Taking Orinha and Ganaha by the hand, she danced with both of them. Her sons then handed over their prisoner. Katari pulled the girl behind her, followed by the other two Erie captives whose lives would be spared. An impressive escort of twenty Iroquois shielded them from the throng. They quickly disappeared behind the bloodthirsty crowd, which now only had eyes for the two remaining prisoners.

Tahonsiwa released the rope holding back his prisoner. "Save yourself, if you can!" he shouted at the terrified woman. Then, Deconissora shoved his prisoner forward, shouting, "Run, you rat! Now my brothers will avenge my wounds!" Blows rained down on the poor prisoners as they tried to inch their way forward. The Mississauga woman fell first, hit by a club that split open her skull. Half dead, she was dragged off to the torture stake. Her suffering did not last much longer. Meanwhile, the Erie prisoner managed, by some miracle, to weave his way through all the obstacles and into the village. It was to everybody's great relief: torturing him would be all the more satisfying.

The festivities continued inside the village, as the members of the war party distributed the rest of the spoils, under the supervision of the grand chief. Nearly every family in the Bear clan received a share of the smoke-cured meat and melted fat. Kondaron's family, which was from the Tortoise clan, received some as well. Orinha gave a deerskin to Katari, another to his sister Assasné, and a second to Conharassan, whom he was eager to spoil. "And here is a scalp for each of you, to give you comfort for the sons and brothers you have lost," he said solemnly. Ganaha gave a basket of corn taken from the Erie to his mother and fine jewels to his sisters. But the finest gift of all was reserved for Oreanoué: a goat-hair headband dyed in bright colours that he tied around the head of his beloved. The scalps he hung over his family's section of the longhouse. Kondaron presented the grand chief with a magnificent sculpted Erie club. (His warriors had agreed to give Kondaron his own richly deserved share of the spoils, despite his protestations.) Then the other warriors handed out their own presents.

Soon, the torture began. Orinha went along to watch, like all the members of the war party and nearly everyone who lived in the village. But he did not get involved, preferring the attentions of Conharassan.

FEAST FOLLOWED FEAST over the next few days. Members of the Bear clan and the Tortoise clan took turns dancing around the scalps the warriors had brought back. The twenty-five victims claimed by Kondaron and his companions, not counting the victims whose scalps they were unable to bring back, continued to be a great source of admiration as they told anyone who would listen. Orinha was no exception; he related his exploits around fires that burned long into the night. Other warriors, back from fighting the powerful Susquehannocks to the south, or Hurons returned to their ancestral lands to the west, had their own tales to tell. But their victories were less clear-cut and therefore less impressive: those warriors returned home with only a handful of scalps and even fewer prisoners. The Susquehannocks had iron weaponry and firearms of their own, making them formidable opponents. Moreover, the former land of the Hurons was now almost deserted. Everyone now dreamed of going off to fight the Erie, to cover themselves in glory of their own. Orinha was invited to join the next campaign to these lands, which was already being planned. Flattered by the honour, he promised to return and spread terror among the Erie, as was his father's wish.

Speaking of his father, the only blot on Orinha's happiness was Garagonké's absence. He still had not returned. Orinha would have loved to tell him about his exploits, to see his eyes light up at his successes and hear his warm words of praise. But no one who'd gone off to fight the Algonquins and the

French at the start of the summer had yet come back. No one had even heard from them. Orinha, so eager to please his father, was deeply disappointed. It weighed on his mind more often than he would have thought possible. Amid all the feasting, Garagonké was sorely missed.

After a week, the village chiefs brought an end to the celebrations, which were upsetting preparations for winter and exhausting provisions. They held one last solemn assembly and handed out presents to honour the most deserving warriors. Kondaron received a brand new musket and a valuable wampum. Orinha, Ganaha, and two warriors who fought the Susquehannocks each received wampum. No other member of the party was so honoured, which filled Orinha with pride. Now he never removed his wampum, just like the village's other proud warriors. Some of the more experienced men nicknamed him "dodcon," meaning "dangerous spirit." Some of them were even a little jealous. But many of the young women looked at him with admiration. Orinha paid no heed to the men who envied him, but the thought of starting a family was becoming more and more appealing. He realized it would be the best way to ensure he had a future in the community.

But first Orinha wanted to trade his beaver pelts with the Dutch. It was the height of the trading season—and high time for him to get involved. He had taken part in the beaver hunt with such enthusiasm that of the one hundred and seventy-five beaver pelts the war party brought back to the village, twenty-one belonged to him. Forty pelts were given to the mother of the Bear clan and another thirty to the mother of the Tortoise clan. The other warriors each received ten pelts, which they could trade as they saw fit with the Dutch.

Orinha was in a hurry to add to the glory of the returning warriors and to own and hand out items from Europe, objects of desire in the village. He knew those objects well: he had used them every day when he lived with the French. He was sure that if he returned to the village laden with cloth, tools, weapons, and metal utensils, he would be able to win the heart of an Iroquois maiden and marry her. He knew now that he could not start a family with Conharassan. She was from the same clan and the Iroquois forbid lasting unions between men and women of the same clan. Despite his disappointment, he wanted to make the most of the interest he was arousing at the moment and find a woman from another clan whom he would be able to marry.

"I can't wait to go to Fort Orange," he told Ganaha one morning, just as Ganaha was leaving once again to see his betrothed, Oreanoué, in the Wolf clan longhouse. "Let's go now, before Iroquois from the other nations bag the best trades!"

"Why the rush, dear brother?" Ganaha answered calmly. "Take the time to savour your victory. You will not always enjoy such high esteem. And don't worry—the Dutch always have everything we could ever want."

"I'm looking forward to getting my hands on all the things my brothers and sisters would love to have. I want to bring them back lots of presents. Don't you want to give Oreanoué the things she dreams of, just like I want to spoil my wife-to-be? Don't you see that Katari can't wait either? She's worried things aren't going to be ready in time for the winter. I'm telling you, now's the time to go to Fort Orange."

"You're wrong about Katari. It's Garagonké she's worried about."

"Exactly! We have to go before Garagonké comes back! Otherwise the celebrations will start up again and winter might sneak up on us. Let's go now!"

Neither Ganaha nor Orinha dared say what they really thought about Garagonké coming home. He was so late they feared that his campaign might have encountered serious trouble. Sometimes they even thought he might never come back: almost all the warriors who'd gone off to war were now back in the village. With Katari growing more anxious by the day, the situation was obviously not normal. And life had become less cheerful around the family fire.

After thinking it over for a moment, Ganaha agreed with Orinha.

"You're right. There are lots of things I'd like to give to Oreanoué. Let's prepare for our trade with the Dutch."

OF ALL THE BEAR CLAN, Otoniata had the most experience in trading with the Dutch. He began preparations, and the clan mothers told him what they needed: cloth and blankets, copper cooking pots, knives, needles, scraper irons, and lots of dried peas to add to the cornmeal reserves. The men had other priorities: iron tomahawks and knives, munitions, and firearms. Two days were all Orinha and Ganaha needed to get ready. To avoid tensions between clans and make negotiations with the Dutch easier, from the start Otoniata decided it would be best if only members of the Bear clan went with him to Fort Orange.

The day before they left, an Iroquois who had gone to war against the Susquehannocks arrived at the village, panting for breath. He had been running non-stop for four days in search of help. On their way back, the Susquehannocks ambushed his group as they were nearing Iroquois territory and had lowered their guard. Their enemies killed two of the party, took one man prisoner, and seriously wounded five others, who could no longer walk. The Iroquois implored his brothers to come help the wounded right away and bring them back to the village. He also wanted to recruit a few warriors to give chase to the Susquehannocks and avenge their humiliating defeat.

Kondaron agreed to go with him right away, at the very least to help the wounded. He helped him recruit warriors from his clan, then from the members of his campaign against the Erie. Katari was dead set against Ganaha and Orinha leaving for war again so long as Garagonké hadn't returned and they still hadn't gone to trade. Orinha was secretly delighted. He was so looking forward to making his long-held dream a reality: he was going to be able to trade at last! Ganaha gave in without a word of complaint, also happy at being able to stay with his beloved. Otasseté agreed to bring the injured back to the village, but refused to go off to war again. For his part, Tahonsiwa willingly joined the group of fourteen warriors who were going to set off after the Susquehannocks and avenge their defeated brothers. Consequently, fewer members of the Bear clan would be setting off to trade the next day. Otoniata would exchange the pelts the last-minute recruits had entrusted to him, along with those from the mothers from the Bear clan.

The next morning, just before the eight members of the trading expedition left the village, more unsettling news reached them. An ambassador from the Iroquois nation of the Onondaga was on his way to announce to the Mohawks that peace talks were underway with the French. One of the ambassador's chiefs had just returned from negotiations in the St. Lawrence Valley. He reported that, of all the Iroquois he met there, no one had seen Garagonké for many weeks. Katari was dismayed by the news. Ganaha and Orinha were worried. But in the face of so much uncertainty, it was best to proceed with the trading expedition as planned.

||||||||||||||||||||||||||||||||||||||||||||||||||||||||||||||||||||||||||||||||||||||||||||

CHAPTER 10

SURPRISES
AT RENSSELAERWYCK

THE IROQUOIS WALKED for two days to reach the first Dutch village, where fewer than one hundred people lived. Otoniata, who knew the settlement well, marched straight into the first house he came to, as if he owned the place. He flung open the kitchen cupboard and grabbed all the food he could find. Then, with one swing of his arm, he flung a stack of wooden bowls and utensils to the floor, threatening the man of the house with his tomahawk when he tried to intervene. Cocksure, he then sat down at the table and started to eat, inviting his companions to do likewise. The other seven Iroquois then began to turn the house upside down for food, picking up whatever caught their eye as they went, leaving nothing in exchange. As though they didn't already have enough to eat, they moved on to the next house to devour everything they could lay their hands on.

Unhappy with what he found, Otoniata continued to fling objects, tools, and utensils to the floor to frighten the Dutch and impress his companions. Men, women, and children cowered in terror at the back of their homes. Even though they outnumbered the Iroquois one hundred to eight, they did not dare to attack these warriors, who were better armed and stronger than they were. Making himself right at home, Orinha helped himself to meat and vegetables from a huge cooking pot hanging over the fire. He bothered no one, and no one stood in his way. Life was simple when you were one of the strongest.

When evening fell, Otoniata at last found what he was looking for: a jug of potent Dutch gin and a small keg of beer hidden under a bed. He cried out in triumph and he and two friends emptied the jug in no time. In frenzy, the three ransacked the house like madmen, fighting each other as they staggered around. Ganaha, Orinha, and the other three Iroquois drank only beer and wreaked less havoc. Orinha felt only a little light-headed and kept well out of the way. He looked on in surprise as the three men he had travelled with—Ganaha, Deconissora, and Thadodaho—pushed and shoved each other clumsily. He had never seen them like this before, even when they were starving with hunger, even when they were injured. Orinha wondered, "What malevolent spirit has taken hold of them? Have the Dutch cast an evil spell? What's in this alcohol that makes them act like this?" He resolved not to let another sip of beer pass his lips. He would keep his wits about him. But then his companions lay down on the floor one by one and were soon sleeping like logs. Thankfully, none of them had hurt themselves. Orinha lay down as well and quickly fell fast asleep.

The next morning, long after the sun had risen, the eight Iroquois slowly gathered together their bundles of beaver pelts. Otoniata and his two drinking companions seemed slowly to be returning from another world. They looked crazed and uncoordinated. The others were faring better, particularly Orinha, who felt stronger and more alert than his companions. In the end, they stole only a few objects from the Dutch, leaving most things where they fell. Then, without saying a word, they departed for Fort Orange. Orinha led the way with

Ganaha, who knew the route. In the evening, they stopped within sight of the smoke rising from the village of Rensselaerwyck. There, cannons protected the villagers and the substantial garrison housed in an impregnable structure: Fort Orange. Otoniata no longer felt like bragging and boasting, and decided to wait until the next day before making contact with the Dutch. His plan was to arrive early in the morning, going from house to house and trading with the villagers first. Then they would move on to Fort Orange, where the commander always welcomed them with open arms.

AT DAWN, the Iroquois put on their war paint to impress the Dutch and strike a better bargain. As soon as they appeared at the edge of the woods, laden down with their heavy bundles of beaver pelts, the villagers came out to meet them. At this time of year, the Dutch were ready to drop whatever they were doing for a piece of the most lucrative business in the Americas: the fur trade. The pelts were worth their weight in gold for the merchants who sent them back to Europe, where they were turned into felt and luxury hats. Ten or twelve villagers were already jostling for favour, inviting the Iroquois into their houses. Some knew a few words of Iroquois, but most gestured wildly, their actions drowned in an incomprehensible flood of Dutch.

Otoniata followed one of them into his home, and the rest of the party trooped in after him. The man and his wife served them treats: bread and prunes from Europe. No stranger to the welcome ritual, Otoniata also called for alcohol. The man agreed and poured a little wine into two terracotta cups, one for Otoniata and one for himself. Then, they raised their cups and drained them in one gulp. Now bargaining could begin.

Since it was his first time, Orinha paid close attention to how the Iroquois and the Dutch traded. The man of the house first laid out four long iron knives on the table and gestured that he wanted two beaver pelts for each. Otoniata shook his head and signalled that he was prepared to give only one pelt per knife, no more. The man screwed up his face in disgust. He moved over to get a closer look at the pelts Otoniata had laid beside him out on the ground. He felt them, shook his head, and held up two fingers. Otoniata stood up abruptly and ordered his companions to follow him out of this den of thieves. The Dutchman cursed himself for setting his sights too high and missing out on a great moneymaking opportunity.

News of their arrival spread like wildfire. The eight Iroquois pushed their way through the small crowd gathered around the door to the first house and moved on to the next, where the Dutch couple who lived there welcomed them like royalty. Beside herself with excitement, the lady of the house hurriedly spread a white cloth over the simple table that occupied the centre of the only room in their little wooden house. Then, in chipped terracotta plates, she served her guests meat from the iron cooking pot hanging over the fire. But the food was not to the Iroquois' liking, except for Orinha, who was surprised to rediscover the taste of salt and pork he'd eaten so often in France and in New France.

The man of the house showed the Iroquois his old musket, while his wife cleared the table with lowered head, eyes half-hidden under her bonnet. She laid a red blanket on the table, which Otoniata, Ganaha, and Thadodaho explored with their hands, giving it their complete attention. The thick cloth was soft to the touch and appeared to be warm and comfortable. Otoniata was the first to offer four beaver pelts for the musket and the blanket. The man jumped back, hiding the musket behind him to show that the offer was too low. He pointed to the blanket with his free hand and held up four fingers, nodding all the while. To make sure he was understood, he then showed the musket again, indicating that he wanted four more pelts for it to be part of the bargain. Otoniata hesitated.

"I'll give you two beaver pelts for the blanket," Ganaha cut in, holding up two fingers.

"I'll give you three for the blanket," Otoniata retorted, "but you can keep your old musket. I have a better one."

Without waiting for the Dutchman's reaction, or for a higher bid from Ganaha, Otoniata grabbed the blanket and began to unpack his furs. He motioned to the man to choose three pelts from the pile. It was a deal, no matter what Ganaha and the Dutchman might have thought. The Dutchman hurriedly took the furs owed to him, rolled them up as fast as he could, and handed them to his wife, who went straight to the back of the house to put them in a wooden chest. Seeing this, Ganaha pointed to the chest the woman had taken the red blanket out of. "Any more blankets?" he asked in Iroquois. "Show me." She understood and pulled a worn old blanket from the chest. Ganaha gave it a half-hearted feel, disappointed, making it clear that it was of no interest to him. Thadodaho piped up to offer her two pelts for it. The man and the woman glanced at each other and accepted his proposal, barely able to suppress a smile.

The Iroquois moved on to another house, where they were again served treats and wine. Some made trades in return for axes and knives. Ganaha snapped up a set of iron needles and glass pearls. "For Oreanoué," he told Orinha. "She'll be so pleased. I also want to bring back some nice blankets and cooking pots and iron utensils for her." It occurred to Orinha that he should do the same thing, and bring back some glass pearls to charm the young ladies of the village. They could decorate their clothes with them. He also wanted to bring back blankets and a big copper cooking pot for Katari.

INSIDE FORT ORANGE, a smartly uniformed soldier climbed the wooden staircase leading to the apartments of Peter Orlaer, the governor and commander of Rensselaerwyck. The soldier knocked and walked right in.

"Good morning, Commander," he said. "The Iroquois have just arrived. There are only eight of them, but they have lots of furs."

Sitting at his desk, the governor was polishing off his breakfast. He stood up slowly, wiping his mouth and hands with his serviette, then asked his lieutenant:

"Do you know them?"

"I recognized Otoniata and Deconissora from the village of Coutu. But I'm not sure I know the others. You can't always tell from this distance."

"Come with me. We'll have a look from the stockade. Do you know which way they came?"

"I imagine they came from the north, Commander."

The governor and the lieutenant walked down the staircase from the main bastion where Peter Orlaer had his apartments and strode over to the fortified enclosure surrounding the buildings.

"They must have crossed the river near Schenectady," the lieutenant said. "That's the best route from their village."

They followed the inside wall of the stockade for a short distance, climbed the ladder in the corner up to the parapet, then looked out through the trees over the northern part of the village of Rensselaerwyck.

"Where are they?" Governor Orlaer asked.

"Over there," replied his lieutenant, "Where the people are gathered outside van Bogaert's house. They're all trying to coax them into their homes."

"The village folk are even greedier than I am. Look at them, vultures," said the governor. "Take two or three men with you and keep a close eye on them. Don't make a scene. Make sure they don't drink too much. I don't want any fuss. Let them trade a few furs with the villagers; then invite them to come and meet me. Tell them I want to make them an offer. See to it that they come up here with plenty of beaver pelts. Go now. I'll prepare one of the receptions they're so fond of."

"Very well, Commander. You can count on me."

No sooner did he walk through the door than Orinha spied the big copper cooking pot hanging over the hearth. He wanted it, but didn't start bargaining right away. All day long, he had seen that the Dutch would do anything to get their hands on their furs. But he still had trouble judging how many pelts their valuables were worth, and he was reluctant to haggle. As in the other houses, he let Otoniata and Deconissora talk to the woman who enticed them into her home by dangling a large piece of cloth from her doorway. She really did have more cloth than any other home they'd been to. She showed them different cuts in red, brown, white, and blue, and lovely ready-to-wear shirts. Her husband stayed back, close to the fireplace, keeping a mistrustful eye on his wife and the Iroquois, ready to step in should the need arise. Their daughter, who must have been eight or nine years old, was cradling a baby in her arms. She stood in front of the wooden counter the family used as a table, stock-still, looking on in fascination as her mother laid out her fabrics for the Iroquois.

Orinha looked around the only room in the house for other items he could combine with the pot to bargain for everything together. His plan was to bring down the price of each. He remembered that was what his father used to do back in France, with great success. He looked at the frame of the building, at its walls, at the rough-hewn furniture, at the everyday objects used by the family and the memories came flooding back. He rediscovered everything that used to be so familiar to him: a table, chairs, a chest, a wooden cupboard, a terracotta jug and plates, iron pans and cooking utensils hanging over the hearth, where the fire was burning away beneath the huge copper pot...

Suddenly, behind the young girl, Orinha caught a glimpse of a knife she must have been using to chop vegetables. It lay half-hidden among bits of cabbage and turnip. Its handle gleamed strangely in the half-light. Orinha took a step closer, then a second, discreetly, so as not to frighten the girl or her parents. Now he could get a better look at the unusually shaped handle. It seemed to be made from some kind of precious substance. In some ways, it seemed so familiar, and yet he had never seen the likes of it before. He edged closer, but this time he drew the attention of the young girl, who moved fearfully toward her father. The knife continued to shine in the dim light of the fire. The blade was long and broad. The handle had been sculpted to resemble the head of an eagle. Orinha was absolutely fascinated by it. Driven by an irrepressible urge, he suddenly seized the knife and said in Iroquois: "I want this knife!" Energy surged through his whole body. Everyone in the house turned and looked at him, surprised by his actions and his tone of voice. "I want this knife and the copper cooking pot that's hanging over the fire," he said again, just as forcefully. "How many pelts do you want for both?"

The Dutchman did not understand Orinha's question. He glanced at his wife, who had broken off negotiations with

Otoniata and Deconissora. She was also surprised by Orinha's tone. Frightened by the knife he now held in his hand, she backed away until she reached her husband and held her daughter and the baby tight in her arms. Orinha picked up his bundle of beaver pelts and set it down between the Dutch couple, motioning for them to help themselves. "I'll give you as many pelts as you like for both," he added suavely, throwing in his broadest smile for good measure. But Otoniata, offended at being interrupted, replied that he wanted the knife too: "I'll give you five pelts," he declared, holding up all five fingers of his open hand. Orinha could not bear to miss out on the eagle-head knife. It fitted the curves of his hand perfectly and filled him with energy. There was no way he could leave without it. He felt invincible, cunning, sure of himself. He addressed the Dutch couple with full composure, and another smile:

"I will give you as many pelts as you want in return for the knife, the copper pot, and this shirt," he added, picking up one of the shirts off the table.

To the Dutch it sounded as though they were getting the better end of the bargain, but again they hesitated, not sure they understood. Otoniata seized on their confusion to try to win the day, laying his last seven beaver pelts out in front of him.

"I'll give you seven pelts for the knife and this blanket," he said. "SEVEN."

Orinha, who still had all his pelts left, more than anyone else in the group, upped the ante. "TEN pelts!" he cried. The only way Otoniata could get the better of him now was if he dared use the furs from the clan mothers. But he remained silent.

Orinha used the precious knife to cut the ties around his beaver pelts and stacked ten of them in front of him. He then worked his way nimbly around the room, picking up a long iron poker and a lovely-looking piece of cloth lying on the table. Looking as affable as ever, he added four more pelts to his offer, pointing to the pot, the poker, the shirt, the piece of cloth, and the knife that was so dear to him. He clasped the knife proudly in his hand, so that everyone could see its eagle-head handle. This time, the offer was clear. The Dutch, grasping and practiced, indicated they wanted two more pelts for the lot. Orinha wasn't taken in.

"Fine. But then I want two handfuls of the glass pearls my brother got from your neighbours. Show them, Ganaha!"

The man and the woman, trying hard to guess what Orinha might be saying, shot each other a questioning look. To try and make himself understood, Orinha used a French word he could still remember: "Rassade." Ganaha showed them the glass pearls. The woman ran off to get some from her neighbour right away. The deal was sealed when she returned. Orinha added the two pelts, as the woman emptied the pot with her daughter, while the father held the baby in his arms. Then, Orinha packed his five remaining pelts into the pot, along with everything else he had just acquired. He kept only the knife on him. Deconissora and Ganaha then exchanged beaver pelts of their own in return for a shirt and a piece of cloth. Otoniata, still piqued, bought nothing. At last, the Iroquois left the house.

Jean, the lieutenant, was relieved to see the Iroquois reappear after having spent so much time in the house. The woman running back and forward to her neighbour's had put him especially on edge. He was surprised to see the Iroquois leave so many pelts behind and decided that it was time to step in, sensing that something out of the ordinary had just happened. A young Iroquois he had never seen before was triumphantly carrying a huge copper pot on his back, and Otoniata was clearly very unhappy indeed. Followed by the three soldiers accompanying him, Jean weaved his way through the villagers of Rensselaerwyck, who were all paying court to the Iroquois. He intercepted them before they went into another home.

"Otoniata, the governor wants to see you," he said to the group's leader in Iroquois. "He is looking forward to hearing your news and has presents for you. He told me you should not delay. It is time for you and your brothers to follow me to the governor's quarters."

Jean had come at the right time. Otoniata, reassured by the lieutenant's intervention, felt important. The soldiers and the Iroquois strode briskly over to the fort, moving the villagers out of their way. The villagers grumbled at the lieutenant for bringing the trading to a close. They knew all too well that the governor would snap up all the remaining furs for himself. Villagers who hadn't yet had a chance to make a deal of their own tried one last time to convince one of the Iroquois to exchange pelts with them, in return for a knife, a musket, a shirt. But in vain. The Iroquois were now gearing up for the most important negotiations of the day.

Orinha was so carried away by what had just happened that he was barely aware of what was going on around him. He feared he had probably dealt away too many pelts in the exchange, but he was overjoyed at getting everything he wanted in return: the cooking pot for Katari, pearls to help coax a woman to marry him, the Dutch shirt he wore with pride. Thinking back, he didn't regret a thing. First and foremost, he had gotten his hands on the wonderful eagle-head knife, the very touch of which against his skin flooded him with energy. Holding the knife in his hand gave him a strange feeling of exaltation, as though a powerful spirit had slipped inside him and was now protecting him and showing him which path to take. Orinha did not really understand what was happening.

The sun was already on its way back down again when the small group reached the entrance to the fort. Jean barked out an order and the gate swung open. Forty soldiers formed a guard of honour for the Iroquois to walk through. The warriors from both sides greeted each other respectfully. Jean then led his guests to a cloth-roof shelter, where Otoniata and his brothers sat down. Peter Orlaer, the governor of Rensselaerwyck and the fort commander, came to meet them moments later, dressed in his finest attire. A sword hung from around his waist and a black kerchief adorned with coloured feathers covered his head, Dutch style. He welcomed his guests in Iroquois, which he spoke very well indeed.

"The Dutch are the Iroquois' best friends. As their chief, I am always happy to welcome you to Fort Orange. As you can see, I have had a cooking pot hung over the fire. Shortly, we will eat to celebrate our business together. There will be plenty of cornmeal and venison for all, for I am fond of my Iroquois brothers and I want them to return home happy after their visit. I hope the friendship between us will be carried on from generation to generation and you will return often to trade with me."

The governor paused, looking each of the Iroquois straight in the eye. His soldiers stood in a semi-circle behind him, giving him an air of even greater prestige and authority. Orlaer went on, pointing to the bundles of beaver pelts.

"I see you have brought many beautiful beaver pelts and I thank you for them. In exchange, I have presents for you that are worthy of the great warriors you are and the efforts you have made to regularly supply us with furs. You understand what makes us happy. I tell you most sincerely, the Iroquois and the Dutch are the best warriors on this earth. God willing, we will never again have to fight each other, as in the past. Let us forget those days gone by, let us never think of them again, for the clash would be terrible indeed. The Dutch have always given you the very best muskets in exchange for your beaver pelts, and you have used them well. But the Dutch are an inventive people. We work hard, and are always striving to improve ourselves. I have just received new muskets, better than any you have ever held in your hands before today. They arrived here after a long and perilous journey across the ocean. The Dutch are many on the other side of the salty sea and have used all their skills to make them. The muskets I am offering you are truly extraordinary. Come with me. Come admire them."

Well-disposed after the governor's flattering speech, the eight Iroquois got to their feet and followed the Dutch commander to a small stone building guarded by some twenty soldiers. Everything had been carefully prepared to impress the Iroquois. The governor ordered the double door to the powder magazine to be opened. Then, five soldiers disappeared inside and soon emerged with thirty muskets, which they swiftly set down against the building's outer wall. The long, polished barrels of the brand new firearms gleamed in the sunshine.

"Here are the muskets I was talking about," the governor announced. "This building also contains all the gunpowder you could ever wish for. Come, come, do not be afraid. Come see all the powder we have for you."

The governor stood back to let the Iroquois peer into the powder magazine through the half-open door. Jean stood by the entrance, ready to block their way should they attempt to enter. Over the shoulders of his brothers, in the half-light, Orinha could make out forty or fifty wooden barrels, big and small. There was enough powder for ten years' worth of fighting! The lieutenant took a closer look at the young Iroquois and noticed that he seemed different to his companions. In the Dutch shirt Orinha was wearing over his Iroquois clothes, he looked very much like a European. He also noticed that Orinha did not react like the other braves. The Iroquois were amazed at the governor's show of strength, but this young warrior was looking coldly at the powder reserves, as though he were sizing up their value, as though he were making calculations.

"Impressive, isn't it?" the governor said. "What you are admiring is probably the most powder you will ever see in all of your lives. Take a good look. The Dutch are powerful and have gathered here all the powder they possess to satisfy your needs and desires. And do not forget, the muskets are the best in the world, better even than the muskets of the French and the English. So, what do you say? Is it not a deal worthy of fearsome warriors such as you? Let us now return to our seats and talk. My soldiers will serve the sagamité we have prepared for you."

Slowly, pensively, Otoniata was the first to return beneath the shelter. He was responsible for trading away almost all the remaining pelts, the pelts entrusted to the group by the clan mothers so they would bring back peas, blankets, and tools. He sat there while his companions lingered a while longer with the muskets, turning them over longingly in their hands, impressed by the long barrels and the shiny new metal while the soldiers kept an eye on them. Orinha continued to peer inside the powder magazine and count the barrels, imagining just how many muskets and cannons could be fired with so much powder. His eyes suddenly met Jean's, who was posted nearby. Orinha smiled. Instinctively, Jean, a Huguenot from France who had fled his country for a new life in the Dutch colony, suddenly cried out in French: "By God! I'll be damned if you're an Iroquois!" Orinha could not believe his ears. He stood there, rooted to the spot.

"By God," the soldier repeated. "Who are you? Speak, stranger! Are you a Frenchman or an Iroquois?"

Orinha, who hadn't heard a word of French for the past eighteen months, was so surprised he could not muster a reply. The soldier knew he'd hit the nail on the head. He grabbed him by the shoulders and asked again:

"Well, I'll be damned if you're not a Frenchman like me! Answer me! Are you French?"

Orinha at last recovered his powers of speech and replied in his mother tongue.

"Yes, I was born in France. But now I am an Iroquois. My brothers adopted me," he said, pointing to his seven companions, who were looking on in astonishment.

The lieutenant let his musket fall to the ground and clasped Orinha in his arms like a long-lost brother, embracing him with all his strength. Orinha, stunned, did not know what to do. Jean was crying. Ganaha and the other Iroquois did not understand what was going on and were starting to show concern. The governor, who also spoke French, realized he must intervene at once.

"Don't worry," he explained to the Iroquois in their language. "My most faithful soldier is thrilled to have recognized your brother, that's all."

Then, he turned to Orinha and asked him if he was indeed French.

"Yes. I was captured in New France, then adopted," Radisson replied in French, amazed at still being able to speak and understand his native language so well after so long.

The governor turned to the Iroquois, who were starting to show their growing confusion and displeasure.

"Don't worry," he told them in Iroquois, "Your brother was just telling us how happy he is to be one of your own. Rejoice and do not be alarmed. I am going off to speak with him for a moment. It is not often that a Frenchman honours your people in such a way and I am eager to hear his story. In the meantime, Otoniata, you shall talk to Jean, my lieutenant. I want all your pelts and I am prepared to be generous. In addition to muskets and powder, you may have as many peas as you can carry to keep your womenfolk happy."

The governor pointed a finger at Otoniata and added sternly: "I have confidence in you, Otoniata. Do not be distracted by my conversation with your brother. Do not miss out on the bargain I am offering you today. I will not always be as generous toward you. Other Iroquois will take me up on my offer if you do not today. Think about it carefully and do not let me down. I will see you soon."

The governor then motioned to Orinha to follow him, telling Jean to finalize the trade with the Iroquois. Orinha and the governor both disappeared into his apartments.

SEATED BEHIND his massive wooden desk, Peter Orlaer looked Orinha straight in the eye and began in French:

"I can help you," he said. "I can buy your freedom, no matter the price. But first tell me how you got here. I want to know who you are."

Orinha was immediately thrown off. He wasn't expecting he would have to speak French. He fumbled for his words for a minute or two. The silence seemed to last an eternity.

"Take your time," the governor added, seeing the young Iroquois' hesitation. "I'm in no rush."

Orinha was very impressed by the attention this powerful and educated man was paying him. The governor knew several languages and lived in this lavish apartment. In all his life, Orinha could not remember ever having visited such a fine apartment, even in Paris when his father rubbed shoulders with merchants richer than himself. An enormous globe mounted in a wooden frame in the middle of the room particularly fascinated him. On it he saw strange animals, huge ships under full sail, and vast painted expanses, adorned with elegant handwriting. He noticed that the legs on the governor's desk were cabled and carved. Behind him, dozens of books looked down from a milled wood bookcase. On one of the walls hung the portrait of a man dressed in sumptuous colours.

Orinha stared at the documents stacked on the governor's desk. He looked in astonishment at his inkwell, his quill pens, a shiny metal pen case—and his French began to come back to him, one word at a time, then more rapidly, building up to an avalanche. As he began to speak, he clutched the handle of his precious eagle-head knife through his clothes.

"My new family saved me from torture because I showed such courage," said Orinha, puffing out his chest. "My brother Ganaha, who is with me here today, captured me in New France. He was the one who wanted to adopt me. He finds me brave and strong. He taught me how to hunt and how to wage war. I went on a long journey with him and our chief Kondaron, to lands far to the west. We claimed victories against the nation of the Erie. I am proud to be an Iroquois. I love my brothers, and they love me too."

Orinha did not know what else to say. He wondered what this man wanted to find out and why he looked so incredulous. All he wanted was to go back to his brothers and finish the trade; it had been going well until now. He was looking forward to returning to the village, to handing out his presents, to understanding what strange power bound him to his new knife.

"Sit down," said the governor. "Don't be shy."

"I'd rather stand," replied Orinha.

"As you wish."

With his piercing stare, Orlaer looked the young Frenchman over with curiosity.

"Tell me about your life in New France," he asked. "Were you born there?"

"I only lived a year in New France," Radisson replied. "I was born in France, near Paris. My French name is Radisson, Pierre-Esprit Radisson, like my father, a merchant. But he disappeared and I came to live with my sisters in New France. My Iroquois name is Orinha. Everyone says I'm worthy of the name. It belonged to the oldest son of my father, Garagonké, and my mother, Katari. He died in battle and I have replaced him."

"Yes, I know the custom. So, is it really true? You enjoy living with the Iroquois?" Orlaer asked, sounding skeptical.

"I love my parents. I love my brothers and sisters. I want to live my life with them. When I go back to the village, I'm going to get married."

Surprised at the young man's assurance, the governor tried to get to the bottom of an attitude that was, to say the least, unusual.

"Do you know how rare it is for a French prisoner to tell me he is happy with the Iroquois? Truth be told, it's the first time I've ever heard a European say such a thing. Normally, they beg me to release them."

"I am no prisoner," replied Orinha. "I am a brave warrior and an excellent hunter. My family is proud of me."

"Very well, you are not a prisoner. Nevertheless, I have the power to buy your freedom, if you so desire. And I can help you find your way home, back to your family. Is that not what you want?"

Troubled by the unexpected possibility that presented itself to him for a second time, Orinha hesitated. The first time, it almost cost him his life. It had been so long since he considered returning to his own people. Now that he had found his way and taken his place among the Iroquois, why would he want to start all over again and go back to New France?

"My mother and my brothers are waiting for me," he said, finally. "My father too. They would all be very disappointed if I did not return to the village. I owe them a lot. They saved my life. I would rather stay with the Iroquois."

The governor could hardly believe his ears. He had no intention of forcing the young man's hand—he said he preferred his new life to life with the Europeans, after all—but he repeated his offer, just to be sure.

"Young man, you astonish me. To be clear: I can deliver you from the clutches of these barbarians. I am prepared to buy your freedom at any price. Tell me what you wish, and I will do it."

Orinha thought it over for just a moment. He had already said he wanted to go on living with the Iroquois, and he had no intention of changing his mind. He was a man of his word.

"I want to see my father Garagonké and tell him of my journey. I want to honour him. He is a great warrior and an admirable man. My destiny is to live with the Iroquois, and I will follow it. Let me leave with them. My brothers are waiting."

In the face of such determination, the governor yielded, though he was no more than half-convinced.

"So be it. If you insist. But you should know that you are choosing a dangerous life for yourself. I admire your courage, but you can always count on me if you ever change your mind. My offer will always be on the table. Let us return to your brothers before they grow impatient, since that is your desire."

As soon as he returned to his companions, Orinha could feel their unease. It seemed that Otoniata had pushed through the trade. They were almost ready to leave: five kegs of powder and three bags of peas had been deposited beside the Iroquois. All the pelts had disappeared, including Orinha's. Soldiers were still making up five lots of muskets. Strangest of all was the clamour from outside the fort. It sounded as though a noisy crowd was pressed against the gate. News of the Frenchman who had become an Iroquois had spread through Rensselaerwyck, and the villagers wanted to see for themselves.

None of the Iroquois asked Orinha what had been said between him and the governor, or explained how they traded the pelts away in his absence. In silence, Ganaha helped him put a small keg of powder and a bag of lead shot into his cooking pot. Orinha said nothing either. The blankets would protect the powder from any bumps and jolts. He was completely weighted down by the heavy load. His companions shared the other kegs among themselves, along with the munitions, the bags of peas, and the twenty-five brand new muskets.

As they were leaving, the governor congratulated the Iroquois on their acquisitions and thanked them for the handsome pelts given in return. As soon as the gate to the fort swung open, one hundred villagers let out a roar, pointing excitedly to the Iroquois, any Iroquois, looking for the Frenchman. Jean walked ahead of the group and pushed the onlookers away with the butt of his musket: "Move away now. Let us through. Stand back." Five more soldiers surrounded the group and cleared a path through the crowd. But the further they progressed into the village, the more villagers there were. Soon, the Iroquois had no choice but to stop and put down their heavy loads to satisfy the curiosity of all those eager to get a glimpse of Radisson, the man they saw as an enigma. They finally spotted him and many were not satisfied until they had touched their fellow European, who was now living as a Wildman. All the soldiers could do was contain the disorder. People spoke to Radisson in Dutch, trying to convince him to stay with them; they pulled on his garments to drag him away from the group. Jean and the other soldiers pushed them away, shouting: "Get back! Get back!" The crowd dispersed, as the onlookers were able to satisfy their curiosity and touch the phenomenon for themselves.

Before Orinha could pick up his load, Jean again held him tight in his arms and whispered to him in French: "It makes me so sad to see you leaving with these barbarians! I will pray for you! Good luck." A woman threw herself into his arms and gave him bread and prunes: "Take these," she said, "they're for you. God keep you!" Then she grasped his face in her hands and kissed him full on the mouth, covering his face with her tears. Orinha—or Radisson, he no longer quite knew who he was—could not take his eyes off the weeping woman who could not bear to see him depart with his brothers. But, mechanically, like his companions, Orinha heaved the heavy load onto his back and left the Dutch village. He walked behind the others, still upset. None of his companions spoke to him, or looked back, until they had disappeared deep into the woods.

It took Orinha two full days to recover. When all was said and done, he was happy to be returning home. He was looking forward to some peace and quiet, and to concentrate on his plans for the future: finding a good wife and trying to clear up the mystery of the eagle-head knife. He hoped to put the intense interlude with the Dutch behind him. His brother Ganaha had also been unsettled by the incident. Since he intended to marry Oreanoué upon his return and move into the Wolf clan longhouse, as custom had it, he reckoned that his adopted brother would just have to get along without him. He no longer wanted the responsibility of always keeping one eye on Orinha; he didn't see the point any more. All the other Iroquois were sure they had just witnessed something very singular indeed. The way the Dutch reacted was going to cause a sensation around the family fire on the long winter evenings to come. They had no doubt that Orinha was one of their own. He was, after all, returning home with them, despite the welcome the governor and the Dutch laid on for him. He had his place among them as a warrior, a hunter, and now a trader; but he was a special case, one of a kind.

||||||||||||||||||||||||||||||||||||||||||||||||||||||||||||||||||||||||||||||||||||||||

CHAPTER 11

ORINHA OR RADISSON?

KATARI HAD BEEN ILL TEMPERED FOR DAYS, sulking with the men and blaming them for bringing back too many weapons from the Dutch. She would have preferred more cloth, more tools, and more food. What's more, too many men from the clan went to war instead of going off to hunt, meaning the women had less food to store away for the winter. Orinha at least did his part, bringing her home a huge copper cooking pot and a poker. He also gave her some of his cloth. But the gifts were not enough. Katari saw that Orinha had become just like all the other men, a proud and arrogant warrior. She was disappointed in him. She had hoped the Frenchman would turn out more like the Jesuit who had stayed in their village and spoke so often of peace. She had thought her adopted son would become an ally to Chief Teharongara, her friend, who was forced out of the village while Orinha was away. His departure infuriated her.

The unfortunate event happened when the Onondaga delegation came to the village to convince the Mohawks to join peace talks with the French. They were not well received. Katari was involved in the discussions, like other clan mothers, and learned that four of the five Iroquois nations wanted to make peace with the French. Only the Mohawks wouldn't budge, refusing to give up the fight.

None of the arguments made by the Onondaga, Chief Teharongara, or the clan mothers cooled the war chiefs' determination to exterminate the French, even at the risk of rupturing the Confederacy of the Five Nations. The clan mothers lamented they could no longer accept so many of their sons dying in battle, especially if the other nations made peace and the Mohawks alone would be left to pay the price. But the arrogant chiefs were set in their ways and drove the clan mothers away from the discussions, paying no heed to tradition. The Onondaga ambassadors did not see fit to stay any longer and left only two days after they arrived. Fearing reprisals, Teharongara the peace chief went with them, such was the venom of those in favour of war.

Katari was so angry that she told the war chiefs in no uncertain terms that a chief like her husband Garagonké would never have been so stupid as to turn the Onondaga ambassadors away. Her outspokenness did not go over well, and they reminded her that she was nothing but an adopted Huron prisoner: their affairs were of no concern of hers. Katari still had not gotten over the whole episode. She had spent her whole life with the Mohawks and sacrificed two of her sons to their passion for war. So, when Otoniata and the other men from her clan brought back such great quantities of muskets and powder, instead of the tools and goods the women had told them they needed first and foremost, Katari flew into a rage against the warriors.

It was clear to Orinha that Garagonké's prolonged absence and the bad news constantly trickling through to them about him had really demoralized Katari. She feared that her husband had finally been lost in battle and that she would again have to pay dearly. She did not speak about it, but Orinha knew that she was beside herself with worry. Orinha, too, was very worried about his father. Again that afternoon, members of a war party from the neighbouring village of Sacandaga had returned from battling the French. They hadn't seen Garagonké in weeks.

EVER SINCE his union with Oreanoué had been confirmed, Ganaha had been spending his time with his fiancée in the Wolf clan longhouse. Orinha had lost his dearest companion. Of the other members of Orinha's war party, Kondaron and Otasseté had not yet returned from the land of the Susquehannocks. Deconissora and Thadodaho had kept their distance since the trading expedition to Rensselaerwyck, and Tahira would spend the winter with the Oneida, after delivering the Erie prisoner to Atotara's family. Only Shononses, who lived beside the fire closest to the space reserved for Orinha's family, in the Bear clan longhouse, spent any time with him at all. Shononses had to take things easy. His arm hadn't healed properly and was still causing him great pain.

"I will never again be able to fire an arrow like I used to," he lamented. "My arm is no longer strong enough. But if you teach me to fire a musket as well as you, I can again be a good hunter."

"I will teach you," Orinha assured him. "You can count on me. I am sure you will again become one of the best hunters we have."

Orinha was reluctant to confide in Shononses, but whom else could he talk to? Who else could he tell about what had intrigued him so since he had returned from Rensselaerwyck? At last, his need to talk to someone got the better of his reluctance to open up.

"I have a question for you," said Orinha, in a serious voice.

"I'm listening."

Orinha could not understand why his eagle-head knife had such an effect on him. He had come to the conclusion that the knife helped him meet his guardian spirit: the eagle. But he was not sure. Since it was not something the Iroquois talked about, Orinha broached the subject in a roundabout way. He took out the knife from under his clothes and showed it to Shononses.

"Take a look at this. I bought it from the Dutch. Have you ever seen a knife like it?"

Shononses was surprised. He picked it up carefully, holding the blade in his right hand and the handle in his left, as though the knife were especially fragile, or dangerous. He took a close look at it.

"What a beautiful knife!" he exclaimed after a moment. "No. I have never seen anything like it."

Shononses turned the knife every which way to admire the sculpted handle. In the middle, right where his hand closed over it, the eagle's feathers were broad and sleek, making it easy to take a firm hold. At the end, the eagle's head and beak were finely drawn, jutting out a little to prevent the hand from slipping. The point where the handle met the broad, solid blade was also beautifully detailed. It was made up of a carved tuft of fine, bristling feathers, forming a small hilt that protected the hand. Shononses could not look away from the eagle's piercing eyes. They seemed so alive. Once he'd managed to break the spell, he asked Orinha:

"Where did you say you got it?"

"From a family in Rensselaerwyck. The women were using it as a kitchen knife. I got it along with the big copper pot that I gave to Katari."

"It's a really nice knife," Shononses said again, admiringly. "It really is. Take good care of it."

"Do you know what the handle's made of?" asked Orinha.

Shononses took an even closer look. He scratched it with his fingernails and touched it with the tip of his tongue. He hefted the handle and the blade in his hand, balancing the knife on his index finger.

"Animal horn," he replied confidently, "but I don't know what kind. I've never seen anything like it. If you ask me, this knife wasn't made by an Iroquois, not by anyone from our nation, at any rate. Not by a Dutchman either. Take really good care of it. It's worth a lot."

Orinha was surprised to learn that the handle came from a foreign land and was probably sculpted by foreign hands. He picked it up again.

"As soon as I saw it, I just knew I had to have it. I couldn't resist. It was as though…"

But he stopped himself just in time, keeping his secret safe, along with the powers of the spirit that in all likelihood lay within the knife. He put his knife away, thanked Shononses, and went for a walk in the forest to mull over the conundrum: it looked as though he had met his guardian spirit through an object that was foreign to the Mohawk nation.

That same evening, around the family fire, Orinha found himself alone with Conharassan and showed her his precious knife. His sister reacted even more enthusiastically than Shononses.

"What a gorgeous knife!" she exclaimed. "Where did you find it?"

"In Rensselaerwyck, on the trading expedition. Listen, Conharassan, I'd like you to make me a nice leather sheath so I can carry it with me everywhere. If you accept, I'll give you the nice red cloth I brought back from the Dutch. It would make me so happy."

"Of course I accept. You know I'd do anything for you. Where do you want to wear it? Around your waist, on your back, across your chest?"

"I want to wear it here, across my chest, hidden beneath my clothes."

The next day, Conharassan went to work. It took her the whole day. Orinha waited beside her the whole time, keeping an eye on his knife and admiring his beloved sister at work. He loved watching her hands move. Meticulously, with no small amount of skill and patience, she cut the pieces of leather and stitched them tight together. She took her measurements directly against Orinha's body to make sure that the sheath would fit perfectly.

By evening, her work was almost done. Orinha was both happy and relieved. He appreciated Conharassan's affection and dedication. Never did he tire of gazing at her radiant face, of the mischievous grin when she softened the leather with her teeth, or her attentiveness as she carefully strengthened the sheath with a second round of stitches. By the flickering light of the fire, he could see her eyes, lit up by her love for him. Orinha would have married her the next day if he had been allowed to marry someone from the same clan. He was sure Conharassan would make a good wife and he would be a good husband. But the laws of the Iroquois forbade it. Orinha was obliged to look elsewhere for the woman of his life, and Conharassan would have to find herself another lover. He had noticed that, for some time, she had been attempting to distance herself from him, encouraged by her older sister, who had no doubt made it clear to her that they had no future together.

Orinha took his knife back before nightfall, but Conharassan refused to hand over the sheath. "I haven't finished yet," she told him. The next day, she added a little pocket. Into it she slipped a delicate shell bracelet from her wrist, along with a lock of her hair.

"To bring you luck," she explained, at last handing the finished product to Orinha. "Your knife is too beautiful to kill.

It will help you find your way in life, perhaps to defend yourself. But it's not a knife for war. Don't forget that. And don't forget your favourite little sister either, who made this sheath with love." Conharassan kissed him. Orinha then slid his powerful eagle-head knife into its precious sheath. He put it on, adjusted it, and then, satisfied, went to find the red cloth to give to his sister, holding her tight in his arms.

ORINHA WAS OUT HUNTING ALONE. Ganaha didn't want to go with him, preferring to stay behind with Oreanoué and his new brothers from the Wolf clan. As he walked through the forest in search of game, Orinha tried to shake off his worries. He wished Garagonké's absence didn't bother him so much, but he couldn't help it. He missed his father dreadfully. After all, he was the reason he became a warrior. He dreamed of telling tales of his victories just to see a father's pride in his son light up his eyes. At the very least, he hoped to regain the affections of his mother, who had taken a sudden dislike to him.

Orinha thought more and more often about the proud answer he had given the Dutch governor. He was no longer certain that he should have reacted as he did. He needed to talk to someone he trusted, like his father, even though he already knew what Garagonké would say to him. But at least he would feel supported, reassured, strengthened in his decision to become an Iroquois. Whereas, right now, he didn't really know. He wanted to feel appreciated again, like when he returned to the village in triumph with his booty and his prisoner. How everyone cheered him.

He thought back often to the face of the French soldier he had met in Rensselaerwyck. How happy he had been to learn that Orinha was French like him, how sad to see him go off with the Iroquois. He could also see the woman who kissed him, her eyes full of tears. He could still taste her warm lips, still hear her cracked voice telling him: "God keep you!" Orinha wondered if they had already forgotten him, or if they still thought of him from time to time, like he thought of them. Here, he might have Conharassan or Maniska to warm his heart, but he could not start a family with one because she was from the same clan, or with the other because she was a slave. It turned out that life in the village was complicated. Everything had been simpler when he was at war. All that had mattered had been sticking together, eating, hiding, killing, surviving.

There was always Sorense, the mysterious woman from the Beaver clan. Of all the young women in the village, Orinha found her the most appealing, the most attractive. He had even begun to court her when he returned from Rensselaerwyck. But he didn't understand her. When he gave her glass pearls and fine cloth, she pushed him away, all the while continuing to throw him the smouldering glances that fired his passion. He remembered word for word what she said to him: "They call you brave, Orinha. But the man I marry must be more than that. Prove to me you are the most courageous, the most daring of all. Go fight the Susquehannocks and bring me back a prisoner. Go alone, fight them alone. If you win, I'll know you are the bravest and I'll do all you desire. I will be yours forever…" Orinha wondered how he could satisfy this woman who intrigued him as much as she attracted him. Why was she provoking him? At any rate, he wasn't so madly in love with her that he intended to risk his life by taking on the Susquehannocks alone. At least, not yet.

PREPARATIONS FOR WINTER were now underway. The able-bodied men hunted, smoked meat, and gathered and chopped firewood. The women brought in the squash crop, storing it at the ends of the longhouses. The corn, hung out in long garlands to dry in the sun, was also stacked high. The cold season was creeping in, and slowing the pace of life.

In the Bear clan longhouse, Otoniata was seriously ill, fighting for his life like a dozen other Iroquois. A shaman from the Tortoise clan had come to drive away the evil spirits that had taken hold of the bodies of the dying. He said, just like Katari, that the Dutch were to blame: they must have cast an evil spell over them. Every trading season brought with it the strange maladies that struck down so many victims, year after year.

Orinha was busy stacking wood at one end of the longhouse when he heard his sisters arguing at the other end. He could hear their raised voices, but couldn't make out what they were saying. By the sound of things, Assasné was taking Conharassan to task. Her sister replied in tears. Suddenly Conharassan pushed her sister out of the way and ran outside. Orinha dropped what he was doing and peered outside to see which direction she went. He decided to follow her from a distance, not knowing what Assasné could have said to so upset her. He walked quickly between the longhouses and followed his sister out of the village. He was not sure whether to keep following her—after all, their quarrels were no concern of his—but when Conharassan stopped at last at the edge of the woods, he made up his mind to console her. Orinha walked up slowly on his sister so as not to frighten her and asked her gently: "Why are you crying, Conharassan?"

At first, she didn't want to reply, or even look at him. She just wiped away her tears with the back of her hand. But her brother insisted, and she turned around in anger:

"You're the reason I'm sad. It's time you told me the truth!"

"What are you talking about, Conharassan?" Orinha shot back. "Tell me. I want to know."

She hesitated for a moment. Then, with an air of defiance, she looked Orinha straight in the eye and told him what Assasné had just repeated to her for the twentieth time.

"My sister says everyone in the Wolf clan knows that you killed Kiwagé's two brothers when you ran away and that you're lying when you say it was the Algonquin. Are they right?"

"That's not true!" retorted Orinha. "I have never killed an Iroquois! Negamabat would have killed me along with the other three if I hadn't gone with him."

"Do you swear?" Conharassan asked, in desperation, and started to cry again.

"I swear!" replied Orinha. "I swear on the heads of Katari and Garagonké who saved my life! I swear on the head of Ganaha, who knows I have killed no one from the village. Ask him. He'll tell you."

"I did ask him," said Conharassan, burrowing into Orinha's arms. "He says that Kiwagé is talking nonsense and that I shouldn't listen to people who say bad things behind your back. But Assasné won't let it go. She wants me to stop talking to you. It's her friend Kehasa's fault. She's Kiwagé's sister."

Orinha held Conharassan in his arms to reassure her, and to reassure himself. This awful story was going to dog him forever! How could he ever turn the page once and for all? How could he be sure for his safety when one of his own sisters was convinced he killed his Iroquois companions? Hadn't he already paid enough for the ill he did that day? Orinha had no choice but to keep the secret to himself.

"Believe me, Conharassan. Don't listen to Assasné or anyone else. They don't know what really happened. They weren't there when the Algonquin killed our brothers. Conharassan,

I promise you I didn't kill any of my companions. I am your brother, a brother to you all. I have risked my life for all of you. Ganaha can tell you how bravely I fought alongside my Mohawk brothers..."

"I know, Orinha. I believe you. It's just Assasné, she won't let it go! I can't bear to hear it any more. I think she's jealous of the two of us."

"Don't worry, Conharassan. Let's forget all about it and go back to the village. One day when Katari is in good spirits, I'll talk to her about it. She'll get Assasné to leave you alone. It'll all work itself out, don't worry."

After bringing Conharassan back home, Orinha stacked another few logs to hide his inner turmoil and anxiety, then wandered over to the Wolf clan, as though nothing had happened. He didn't know exactly who Kiwagé and Kehasa were, although he thought he might have seen Kehasa a few times with Assasné.

After lingering for a long time outside the Wolf clan longhouse without seeing anyone, Orinha barged right in, ready to say he urgently needed to speak to Ganaha, if anyone asked what he was doing there. Ever since he had been captured and brought back to the village a second time, he hadn't set foot inside this longhouse, where he knew he had no friends. Now, on learning that he probably had enemies there, he wanted to see their faces and gauge how much of a danger they were to him.

Orinha burst into the longhouse and took a few steps through the half-darkness before a young man stepped in front of him and asked him, in a threatening voice:

"What are *you* doing here?"

"I've come to speak to Ganaha. It's urgent."

"Use the other door. Ganaha lives at the other end of the house. You have no business here. Get out!"

Orinha's eyes quickly adjusted to the darkness. Now he could make out a handful of people gathered around the dying embers of a family fire. He called over to Kehasa.

"What is it?" asked one of the young women, turning in his direction.

Orinha recognized Assasné's friend.

"Assasné wants to see you," added Orinha, who, at the very same moment, shuddered with surprise to see his heart's desire, Sorense, stand up too.

Sorense had been chatting with Kehasa when she heard Orinha's voice. Now she stood before him, casting the smouldering looks that bewitched him so. Then, without warning, she turned around and dashed to the other end of the house. Orinha walked around the young man standing in his way to go follow her and ask her what she was doing here when another man grabbed his arm.

"Stop!" he hissed. "You deaf, Orinha? Get out of here now! And don't make us say it a third time..."

Orinha wasn't used to being threatened like this. He turned around to stand up to the man who gripped his arm so tightly he wanted to cry out in pain. He vaguely recognized his face, and suddenly panicked. Pain shot across his body, and a wave of horror engulfed him. The first young man caught hold of him again and said:

"Do what Kiwagé says, you dirty French pig. If you want to see Ganaha, go round the other end. Now get out!"

Orinha could no longer speak. Could barely breathe. Sweat was pouring down his back. Without any fuss, he backed out slowly, forcing himself to keep his fear under control. He hurt as though he had just been struck by lightning. Orinha's only thought was to get back home as fast as he could, limping slightly, as though a stone had just shattered his right foot, as though he had just been battered from head to toe. He walked on, gasping for breath, the feeling that he was being followed preying on his mind. At last, he entered the house of the Bear, where he felt safe. He hobbled over to his bed and lay down. Terrible images exploded in his head; his heart was pounding in his chest; he could see himself in hell. Little by little, he managed to calm down, to capture some of the thoughts that were spinning through his head. The face and voice, he was almost certain now, belonged to the man who had plunged the red-hot sword into him when he was being tortured. He was his most vengeful torturer, almost certainly a brother to one of the young Iroquois from the Wolf clan that Negamabat and he murdered.

Kiwagé had not forgiven him and was out for revenge. He wanted Orinha—he wanted *Radisson*—to die to make up for the death of his brothers. And his sister Kehasa wanted the very same thing. She had even convinced Assasné that her adopted brother was a murderer, and now Assasné was pestering Conharassan to have nothing more to do with him. And to think that Ganaha now lived over there with them! When would *he* turn against him too? How long would it be before his mother Katari also turned against her adopted son, the son who had dashed her hopes by choosing war over peace? When would they decide to put this Frenchman to death for casting the evil spells the Iroquois so hated? Even in the house of his clan, even no more than two feet from the family fire, Orinha still felt threatened.

But the cruellest pain of all came from Sorense's sultry glances, burning only with the desire to see him dead. "Go fight the Susquehannocks alone," she said. "Prove to me you are the most daring of all... If you win, I will be yours forever..." Nothing but a trap. Orinha could now see right through her sinister words: "Love me and I will put an end to your days..." What bitter deceit! He didn't know what made her act as she did. Out of love for Kiwagé? Out of sheer cruelty, perhaps, or the simple lust for revenge. He felt terribly vulnerable to her and the other village women. How could he defend himself against blind love? Then another thought hit him: What if the whole village wanted him dead and was busy planning his torture? He had to fight to keep his panic in check. Fleeing that very minute wasn't an option. He was not ready; it would be too dangerous. If he did run away, he would have to prepare his escape. Otherwise, he would be tortured to death.

Only Garagonké could bring an end to the uncertainty. But he was not there. Where was he? When would he return?

ORINHA WAS OVERJOYED to see his father again. He found him in the woods after a long search. Garagonké was lying in a clearing, beneath the magnificent trees. He looked as though he was asleep, but his eyes were wide open and he smiled at his adopted son. As he drew closer, Orinha noticed a thin trickle of blood running from Garagonké's half-open mouth. But he was not in pain. Garagonké smiled at him and motioned for him to come closer. Orinha came closer. Gently he raised the old warrior's head and cradled it in his arms. Both were silent for a long time. Songbirds flitted between the spreading boughs, the river water babbled in the dazzling sunlight. Orinha realized his father was dead; in his arms he held his spirit. Garagonké looked so peaceful, his body giving off a blinding light from another world. The father looked intensely at his son. His warm, strong breath overcame Orinha: Garagonké was about to speak. He saw his lips move. Suddenly, his voice boomed out over all the other sounds of creation, echoing like thunder. "My son, listen to the message I must entrust to you before I join my ancestors."

Orinha leaned forward to listen to Garagonké's words.

"I was a great warrior," he told him. "Many moons from our village, women would hide and children would cry at the sound of my name. Warriors feared my strength, my courage, and my cunning. But this is not the path for you, my son. I have seen you fight and I know that you do not love war as I loved it. The spirits will lead you down another route. Listen to the voice of the eagle. It will carry you far from the Iroquois.

"Deganawida beseeched us to bring together all the peoples of the earth under the great tree of peace. But I misunderstood him. The troubled times we live in muddled my heart. War intoxicated me. But you are not from our nation; you must not avenge our ancestors. I implore you to first look for peace before you fan the flames of war. Peace takes more time and courage than war, but you must conquer it. I am asking you to bring us peace. That is how you will honour my memory."

Garagonké fell silent. His eyes were transformed into two lightning bolts; his body became light as air. Orinha felt nothing more than a breath brush against his face and stir his mind. Garagonké had vanished.

Orinha stayed there, alone. The clearing was flooded with blinding light. Then he was lifted high up into the air, swept away, gliding over an immense lake.

Suddenly he was back on his bed of fresh pine. Orinha tried to protect his dazzled eyes, shielding them with his arms. It was a rude awakening. Yet all was calm in the dark longhouse, where his brothers and sisters slept on in silence. Slowly, he recovered his breath and realized that Garagonké had appeared to him in a dream. He remembered his words and again saw his spirit soaring toward the land of his ancestors.

It was the middle of the night, but Orinha could no longer sleep. He got up noiselessly, so as not to wake anyone, and crept outside. The night was fresh and cool. The purest of skies was bursting with shimmering stars. He breathed in the cool air that told of the coming of winter. But he was not cold. Or afraid. He knew now that Garagonké was dead. He would wait for him no more. He would never see him again. He would only regret not being able to tell him of his exploits, not being able to feel the happiness that came with hearing him say: "I am proud of you, my son!" But Garagonké was asking him to take another path, the path of peace, as Katari had hoped, as Conharassan had seen in the beauty of his eagle head knife.

All things considered, no one could protect him now from the vengeance smouldering in the hearts of Kiwagé and his Iroquois friends. Orinha realized he could no longer live in the village in safety. All he could do was make his escape.

ORINHA SLEPT SOUNDLY until the early hours of the morning. When he awakened, he looked up from his bed to see Katari blowing on the embers and stirring them with the poker he gave her, bringing the family fire back to life. The longhouse was quiet, still dark. No hurry, no worries. It seemed very much like happiness. Little by little, the other mothers lit their family fires in turn, and soon all the fires ran in a straight line through the spacious bark dwelling. Orinha loved this time of the morning when all was quiet. He admired his mother, always the first out of bed, despite her age and her worries, always alert and generous, ready to bring warmth and light to everyone as soon as they got up. Maniska was now by her side, discreet and efficient. Orinha was glad he had saved her life. She had proved a big help to Katari, who was good to her, even though she was a slave.

Beside them, Shononses had gotten up. He moved closer to the neighbouring fire to warm himself, calm despite the injury that had handicapped him. Every time Orinha saw him, he remembered their extraordinary journey together. At that very moment, he was happy to be an Iroquois. He would have liked to stay with them, if his community had been calmer and less violent. But vengeance smouldered there like the embers of a fire, and it would take very little to rekindle it. The burning flames of hatred would consume all in their path. Orinha knew that he must leave.

He patiently did his best to untie the knot that formed in his stomach at the very thought of running away. He took the time to tame the fear that clouded his mind and made him loose his self-assurance. He focused on the idea that was starting to form, anchoring it firmly in his mind and body, so that he would be able to carry it through, just as surely as an arrow flies through the air. Orinha did not want to take any risks. He would not mention a word of his dream to Katari. She would understand it right away. She would be convinced that her husband was dead, more certainly than if his lifeless body had been laid at her feet. Because Garagonké's spirit spoke forcefully, without hesitation, and its message was clear: Garagonké had departed his family for the next world.

As he turned over in his bed, Orinha felt the eagle-head knife. It was sending him the same message as his father. Shononses had been adamant: the hand of an Iroquois had not made the knife and the material for its extraordinary handle didn't come from this part of the world. Garagonké was right. Through the knife, the cry of the eagle was calling him to flee far away. Orinha first wanted to reach the Dutch, where the governor had promised him deliverance; then he would follow his destiny.

Everyone was going about their business. The four women of the family had left Orinha to laze in bed. He got up quietly and rummaged through the things his father had left behind. He found his tobacco supply, took a pinch and slipped it into his knife sheath, alongside Conharassan's bracelet and hair.

Then he picked a few crumbs of cornmeal from Katari's mortar and put them in the sheath too. It was not much, but it would always remind Orinha of the people who saved his life.

The time had come for Orinha to put his plan into action. The bright sunshine gave him courage. He found Shononses sitting outside in the sun, playing his favourite game of chance with other men from the Bear clan.

"I'm going hunting, but not far," Orinha told him. "Tomorrow, if you like, I'll teach you how to become a better shot."

"Great idea!" said Shononses with a smile. "I'll work on my luck today and my shooting skills tomorrow. With your advice, I'll be the best marksman in the village! Better watch out, Orinha!"

"Come off it! If you think you're going to get the better of me that easily. I have a reputation to defend. Start by winning your game today and we'll see if you can beat me tomorrow!"

"Sure. Now let me concentrate. We'll see who comes out on top tomorrow."

"See you later."

Orinha then went to see Katari, Maniska, Conharassan, and Assasné. They were gathered around the big cooking pot he had brought back from the Dutch, preparing a huge batch of sagamité.

"I'll be out hunting all day, mother. Don't expect me back before this evening."

"Eat something first," Katari replied, without looking up, in the sad voice that had become her wont. "Otoniata died this morning," she added after a moment. "I hope you didn't spend so long in bed yesterday because you're not feeling well…"

"No, mother. I'm fine."

Orinha didn't know what to say about Otoniata. Maniska served him a helping of sagamité in a bark bowl, showing none of the affection she still felt for the man who had saved her. Orinha ate in silence as his two sisters bustled around the fire. Busily, they chopped the meat, threw it into the kettle, poked the fire, and stirred the sagamité. Orinha could see that Conharassan felt uncomfortable. She didn't quite know how to act around him when her sister was present. So he hurried to finish his meal.

"Mother, I promise you we will want for nothing this winter. I will do everything in my power to hunt as much as I can and satisfy all our needs."

"Thank you," she said, this time looking him straight in the eye. "But that is not what is worrying me, son."

Orinha knew exactly what was eating away at his mother. He could see in her eyes the disappointment of losing loved ones, made worse by the fact she could not protect them against illness, vengeance, and war that showed no signs of abating. She suspected that Garagonké was dead. Orinha could feel it. And he was sad to see her so downcast, knowing that his leaving would soon add to her sorrow. He felt as though he ought to encourage her once last time.

"Don't worry, mother. Garagonké will be home soon. Don't lose heart!"

"May the spirits hear you my son. May they sustain my husband and us all, just like they once did."

Orinha could not endure any more.

"I'll be back at the end of the day, mother. Don't worry."

He got to his feet. And left.

"Good luck!" Conharassan shouted after him, with her brightest smile.

Their eyes met for an instant, but their love was not to be. Orinha turned around and walked quickly away. He could not wait to get out of the village. But he couldn't leave without seeing Ganaha one last time. He made a stop at the Wolf clan longhouse. Just seeing it set him trembling with fear. But there was nothing for it: he had to overcome his fear. He entered the house at the right end and spotted his brother.

"Welcome!" exclaimed Ganaha when he saw him coming. "Come smoke with me. It's been so long since we spent time together."

Ganaha was pleased to show him the chores he had almost completed: the bed frames and storage space he had replaced, the leaky bark roof that he was busy repairing.

"If we're going to be comfortable this winter, I have to finish patching the roof before the first snow," Ganaha explained. "Sit with me, brother."

Orinha saw how wrong he was to be angry with his brother. He hadn't let him down, after all. All he wanted to do was make Oreanoué's family happy before he married her. He was a good man, always bursting with energy. Orinha could see in Ganaha's eyes, and in the eyes of Oreanoué who was hovering behind him, that they were happy together.

Orinha was happy to see him, but stayed on his guard, despite the warm welcome. He sat facing the far end of the house, in case Kiwagé or another adversary suddenly appeared to turn him in and capture him. He was ready to make tracks at any moment. Now that he was ready to escape, why take any chances? He barely listened to Ganaha. His good sense was telling him to flee the village now, forever. He had believed he was at home here, but now he felt under threat, even in the company of his beloved brother. He tried his best to enjoy Ganaha's company one last time, but the thought that his enemies were perhaps conspiring to bring him down at this very moment weighed on him so heavily that he could not take it any longer.

"I have to go now if I want to get in a good day's hunting," he interrupted. "Can you give me an arrow to bring me luck?"

Surprised at his brother's behaviour, Ganaha took a while to reply.

"Sure. Take whichever one you like. But a good hunter like you doesn't need one of my arrows to bring him luck. This winter, we'll go hunting big game together, far away, just as soon as I finish my work here. Ontonrora will come with us."

At the sound of his name, Oreanoué's brother came in round the back of the house and sat down with them. Orinha's heart exploded with surprise and panic. But he kept his composure.

"We'll bring Shononses too," he managed to add, between two sharp breaths.

"If you like, Shononses will come too, brother. We'll be a team, just like before."

Orinha stood up to choose an arrow at random, then walked to the door, looking nervously from side to side.

"I must go, Ganaha. See you!"

"Come back whenever you want, brother. You are always welcome here."

"Be happy, the pair of you!"

Orinha hurried to the village gate, turning around more than once to make sure that no one was following him. Everything was fine. The coast was clear. Once outside the village, he paused for a moment to make certain that he had his precious knife, a tomahawk, bow and arrows, and musket. He'd taken nothing to eat, lest people think he was trying to run away should he be captured again. Orinha then snapped Ganaha's arrow, keeping only the head, which he slipped into his knife sheath, along with the tobacco, the corn, and Conharassan's hair and bracelet. Before disappearing deep into the woods, he looked back one last time. It was over. Moving rapidly, he headed for Fort Orange.

ORINHA QUICKLY left the trail that led to Rensselaerwyck and cut through the woods. The going would be tougher but safer, since there was less risk of encountering Iroquois off to trade with the Dutch. He moved as fast as he could and soon discarded his bow and arrows. They were catching on the branches and slowing him down. He bounded over fallen trees, hacked his way through brushwood, barged on through bushes, scratching his face and arms, and ripping his clothing as he went, but he did not slow down. The sun was his guide. On he ran for a long time. When he could run no more, he slowed to a walk. But, without fail, images of torture quickly resurfaced and he began to run again, as frenetically as before. His musket was weighing him down and he cast it away. Reaching Rensselaerwyck as fast as he could was all that mattered. He clutched the eagle head knife in one hand to give him strength and wielded his tomahawk with the other to hack his way through the vegetation that blocked his path to freedom. From time to time he paused, panting, exhausted, took his bearings from the setting sun, and then set off again.

His legs were weak, his lungs on fire, his arms bleeding; the approaching night meant nothing. His will to live drove him on. The Iroquois in him kept him moving. Courage and self-denial, strength and endurance—all the qualities he'd learned from his Iroquois brothers were leading him to a new world. But now he was struggling to make any progress at all. The moon, pale and hesitant, had replaced the sun. Orinha tripped over something he had not seen and fell flat on the ground. Unable to get up, he crawled over to a huge, protective tree stump and curled up against it, clinging tightly to the handle of his hope-filled knife. He fell into a deep sleep.

The cold awoke him as the first glimmer of day lit up the immense forest. Orinha was hungry enough to eat a bear. He hurt all over. But suddenly the thought of red-hot irons against his skin had him leaping to his feet. He set out at top speed toward Fort Orange, thinking about his family; no doubt they would be worried about him. Perhaps they'd already started to look for him. No doubt Kiwagé would be calling him a traitor and demanding he be executed. There wasn't a minute to lose. Quick! Run to Fort Orange. Quicker than that! He would fling himself at the governor's feet and remind him of his promise. He would beg for his salvation. He leaped! He jumped! He stumbled! Orinha picked himself up and kept on going. Fatigue was a caress compared to torture. Exhaustion was a soothing balm compared to death.

At the end of that second frantic day, in the half-light that had come over the forest as the sun went down, Orinha at last heard the sound of an axe in the distance. He drew closer, and could make out through the sparse fall leaves a Dutchman cutting down a tree. Orinha inched closer, stealthily, unsure, happy, undecided. Could he trust a man he had never seen before? Should he continue on to the fort? Was this stranger his saviour or the traitor who would ruin all his efforts? Orinha did not have the strength to go on. At this rate he might never reach the fort, and the Iroquois would perhaps catch up with him that same night or early the next morning. So, shaking with hunger and fatigue, he shouted out to the Dutchman:

"Hullo there!"

The man stopped what he was doing and peered into the woods, where he saw an Iroquois gesturing at him wildly. Although he seemed harmless enough, he had an odd look about him. The Dutchman motioned for him to come closer, gripping his axe, ready to defend himself. But the thought of the furs he might be able to trade flashed through his mind. That was certainly worth a risk or two. So, Orinha approached, distrustful himself, holding no weapon, arms outstretched in a sign of friendship. In no more than a few seconds, looks were exchanged and the two men gained a little confidence in each other. Orinha made it clear with gestures that he was prepared to trade pelts, repeating the word "beaver" in Iroquois and in French. Then he pointed to the Dutchman's home. The man agreed to bring him in. But Orinha took fright again and first wanted to make sure there were no Iroquois there, gesturing again and again to make himself understood. The Dutchman suspected what he might be asking and shook his head a number of times. Completely worn out, Orinha followed him into his home. Come what may.

The Dutchman's wife gave the Iroquois something to eat, even though he had the look of a hunted animal and his scratched face and arms inspired more fear than confidence. He looked exhausted, and devoured everything she put in front of him. Orinha regained a little of his strength and somehow got the couple to understand that he had an urgent message for the governor of Fort Orange. This half-reassured them. Orinha asked for something to write with and the man, who couldn't quite believe it, brought him a quill, ink, and paper because, as good Protestants, they could read the Bible and write as well. They were fascinated to see the Iroquois scribble a few words: "Sir, I am the Frenchman you wished to free from the Iroquois. I have escaped. I am hiding in the home of the man who brought you this message. Please set me free before my brothers kill me! Radisson." Then he handed the scrap of paper to the Dutchman and implored him to take it to the governor immediately.

Tempted by what might be in it for him, the man agreed to leave without delay, even though night had fallen. His wife, reassured by the fact that Orinha knew how to write and had a message for the governor himself, was soon trying to soothe him, in the hopes of a better trade. But Orinha heard Iroquois chanting in the distance and was filled with terror. He managed to get the woman to understand that his brothers would kill him if they found him there, because he had chosen to live with the Dutch rather than with them. She helped him hide under the sacks of corn she and her husband had stored away for the winter, at the back of their only room. Orinha hid there, shaking with fear until the man of the house returned with three companions. Jean, the French lieutenant, was one of them. He brought clothes so they could disguise Orinha as a Dutchman. Orinha got dressed in no time, then the four of them hurried off to the fort. They arrived safe and sound, just before dawn.

||||||||||||||||||||||||||||||||||||||||||||||||||||||||||||||||||||||||||||||||||||||||||||||||||||

CHAPTER 12

A NEW LIFE

THE NEXT DAY, Radisson met the governor of Fort Orange in the apartments that had so impressed him the first time. This time around, he felt more at home there, and safe. But he was still not entirely over his anxiety, his frantic flight, or his sudden decision to run away from the Iroquois and save his life. His memories of Ganaha, Katari, Conharassan, and so many other companions were still intense.

What's more, Radisson felt a little ashamed to be standing in front of the governor, who had sized up the situation so well. He was ashamed of being naïve and proud when he had dismissed out of hand the governor's offer to free him right there and then. The two men stood face to face. Radisson did not dare speak first; the governor finally broke the silence.

"I am happy to see you again safe and sound," he said. "I am glad you saw sense, for any foreigner living with the Iroquois is taking a great risk. You never know what mood they're going to be in, what dream they're going to listen to next. The Iroquois are so bellicose and unpredictable that just about anything can happen. My predecessors learned that at their cost."

Radisson said nothing. He knew the governor was right. But he was still very much attached to the ways of the Iroquois, particularly the dreams that had just guided him to Rensselaerwyck. True, a flash of reason had convinced him to come back to his own culture, but he was still not used to it. He had so enjoyed his life with the Iroquois at times that he was reluctant to accept what Orlaer was saying. But he savoured every second of silence in this sumptuous room, in this apartment protected by solid stone walls, beneath a heavy plank roof, furnished with so many sophisticated objects, each a sign of superior European know-how. Radisson had no doubt that the spirit of the eagle had led him to the right place. He was happy and relieved to have made the right decision. All that remained was to adapt to his new life, once again; to adapt to the new life that had once been his own.

"Yesterday," the governor continued, "I redeemed a Jesuit priest the Iroquois captured on the St. Lawrence. Did you know?" Radisson shook his head. "He's a Frenchman like you. I didn't free him because of any fondness for the Jesuits, far from it, but from time to time the Iroquois capture them, and I don't think twice about buying their freedom. These soldiers of the pope are worth it. They're out here risking their lives, preaching the Gospel to the Wildmen in hostile lands. I'll introduce you. I'm sure you'll get along famously. He is still rather upset by the whole episode. They tortured him. You'll never hear him say he enjoyed his time with the Iroquois, as you told me you did. I'm sure you'll have plenty to talk about."

Radisson kept his silence for the moment, unable to find common ground between his affection for the Iroquois and the distant attitude of the governor, who had had an entirely different story when the Iroquois met with him for trade. Nevertheless, he was happy he would soon have the chance to meet a Frenchman who had lived in New France—if his mother tongue ever came back to him. Because, although Radisson understood every word the governor said, his speech was still a prisoner. It was as though it had been put on hold, bound to his thoughts. Orlaer tired of waiting for Radisson's reply and returned to sit behind his desk.

"I'll make both of you the same offer," he announced. "The navigation season is nearing an end. Since I don't intend on keeping either of you here for the winter—that would be unwise—I suggest you both board the boat that leaves Rensselaerwyck for Manhattan the day after tomorrow. You will remain in the hold well out of the Iroquois' sight, in case they get it into their heads to capture you again. Once you reach Manhattan, you will make your way to Holland by merchant ship. I will pay for your passage that far. After that, you will have to get by on your own. I am not in the least bit worried about the Jesuit: those people have friends everywhere, enemies too. But you are from Paris; I'm not sure about you. Try to get along with him. Perhaps he will help you get back to Paris, where you still have family, I imagine. If the Jesuits are half as charitable as they claim, it's the least he can do for you. What do you say?"

Radisson nodded slightly to thank the governor. Then he replied:

"I would have preferred to go straight to New France, Governor. But I accept your offer."

"No boats go to New France this late in the season," Orlaer replied. "There is too much ice on the river. And don't even think about travelling by land! Much too dangerous. You'd either be captured again or you'd die of cold and exhaustion. Don't you want to see your family again?"

"My two sisters are in Trois-Rivières," replied Radisson, "and my father has disappeared. Only my mother still lives in Paris. I will go back to her. I am very grateful to you, Governor."

"Excellent. Then that is how we shall proceed. Jean will take care of you now. I have work to do."

Radisson wanted to pay back his debt to the governor, and made him an offer.

"I would like to give you my tomahawk to thank you for saving my life. It's all I have."

"Keep your tomahawk, young man! I have no need of it, and I will not accept a thing in return for your liberty. You cost me nothing. Unlike that Jesuit. He cost me a pretty penny. I am glad you made the right decision. Glad, too, that I was able to deliver you from the Iroquois. That is all I need."

The governor got up to open the door. The conversation was over.

"Jean will give you all you need. He will also introduce you to the Jesuit. God keep you, young man."

RADISSON WAS NOW DRESSED in a shirt, pants, jacket, hat, and clogs. He had been transformed into a European, from head to toe. Jean introduced him to Father Joseph Poncet, who had arrived in New France while Radisson was off fighting the Erie. The Iroquois kidnapped him while he was travelling between Québec and Montréal with a group of Algonquins. Father Poncet had spent three months in a Mohawk village that Radisson had never heard of. He had been deeply scarred by his stay there. He still wore the same robe he had been wearing when he was captured. He hadn't taken it off since. Though it was now threadbare and torn in places, it was precious to Poncet. He even refused to wear the Dutch clothes the governor offered him, as though the robe protected him, as though it proved he was still someone.

Radisson and Poncet hid in the cook's bedroom, on the first floor of the bastion, where the governor and five officers from the garrison slept. The two Frenchmen got to know each other as they waited for the boat that would take them to Manhattan. Poncet was eager to tell Radisson all about the torture he had suffered. He poured his heart out, seemingly bringing relief to the torments that haunted him still. His eyes were horrified, white with fear, as he showed Radisson where the Iroquois hacked off the index finger on his left hand. It was the only real torture he had endured. It had lasted for only a few hours, so as not to anger the powerful spirits the French sorcerers claimed to follow. But Poncet was still traumatized. He had still not recovered from the ordeal of his brief detention. It was as though by losing a finger, his freedom, and his role as a missionary, he had also lost all courage, all dignity, all meaning in his life.

Poncet had come to New France to convert the Indians, to bring them eternal salvation. But he never was able to achieve the objective he had set for himself as he prepared for the journey in the monasteries of France. He kept singing the praises of the governor, who hadn't thought twice about purchasing his freedom when an old woman came to Fort Orange and used him to pay for goods.

Radisson told him of his own torture, which was much longer and more terrible, even though it had left no lasting scars. For the moment, Radisson did not dare tell the Jesuit of the extent to which he fitted into Iroquois life, to the point where he had fought by their side. He did not think Poncet would understand.

They spend the first night together alone—the cook was avoiding them—and Radisson could barely sleep. He felt partly relieved at describing his torture, but overwhelmed by so many emotions and questions. All Poncet's talk had brought his culture and values to the forefront of his mind, suddenly reducing his experience of Iroquois culture to one of cruelty and pain. He felt the need to say more, to clear his mind. Radisson realized he had killed. Among his victims was young Serontatié whom he would never forget—and who had completely changed his destiny.

The next morning, remembering that priests had the power to forgive sins, Radisson finally overcame his apprehension and asked Father Poncet to hear his confession.

"I have so many things to be forgiven for, Father," he told him.

Poncet, who was already sympathetic to the young man, found in the call of a lost sheep a little of his dignity as a man of God. He perked up immediately. He felt flattered, almost rewarded, and joyfully agreed to grant the sacrament given to him by the Holy Church after years of study.

"I am listening, my son," he replied, joining his hands together. "Kneel down at my feet and confess without fear, for God our merciful Father hears you through me."

What was happening? Why did Radisson suddenly feel the need to wash his conscience clean? He could not explain it. But a barrier had given way inside him, a barrier raised long ago to allow him to live a normal life with the Iroquois. It all came out at once, everything since he was captured: the guilt he felt over his friends' death, the encounter with Negamabat and Serontatié's murder, the number of Erie he killed. He asked for forgiveness for all his sins, which he bitterly regretted. He sobbed at the feet of the stunned priest.

Poncet could not get over the disconcerting confession. He, too, was moved to tears upon hearing the ordeals of the poor young Frenchman. Fate had been so cruel to him.

"Forgive me, Father," Radisson begged. "Please forgive me."

Father Poncet felt a lump in his throat. He could see how fully Radisson had lived as an Iroquois, astonished to see the lengths to which the young man had gone to be accepted by a group that the priest had never understood.

"Do you regret your actions?" he asked finally, hesitantly.

"Oh yes, Father, I regret them! I wish no one had ever died through my own fault, or by my hand. Forgive me; please forgive me. I didn't want them to die!"

Poncet took a deep breath. He had found the purpose of his mission in Canada and his vocation as a priest. He said to Radisson in a more assured voice, in a more solemn tone:

"God forgives you, my son. Of that there is no doubt. By the powers vested in me, in the name of God the Father, I absolve you of your sins. Your sins are now forgiven. Go in peace, my son, and sin no more."

The next morning Radisson felt better, calmer. He better understood the change in life he was again experiencing. For his part, Father Poncet was beginning to realize just how exceptional an experience Radisson's time among the Iroquois had been. As they shared breakfast, the Jesuit asked the young Frenchman, the young, *wild* Frenchman:

"Do you speak Iroquois fluently then?"

"As well as I speak French," Radisson replied. Listen to this…"

Radisson described in Iroquois the longhouse he lived in for more than a year, then what his mother, father, brother, and favourite sister were like. He told the priest of his first hunting trip with Ganaha, when they killed the great bear. He told him of the great courage and wisdom of Kondaron, who led them right to the ends of the earth to vanquish the Erie, and safely back again through the mountains. He told him how extraordinarily skilful the Iroquois were, how they could fashion canoes from bark and then steer them through the most dangerous of rapids. He told him of the almost unimaginable endurance of their warriors, of their cunning, and their fighting skills. He told him of his admiration for the women who worked in the fields and around the house while the men were off hunting and fishing; who even sat on councils alongside the men. He told him how much they all knew about plants. He told him of the eloquent chiefs that spoke, one after another, to prepare for war or peace. He even told him of the rumours making the rounds of the village just before he left, that peace with the French might be about to break out.

Radisson had mixed feelings. By giving such a spirited account of his time there, Radisson locked these precious memories in his mind, where they were going to crystallize now that he had turned his back on his family and his clan brothers. He was still sad to have left them, but he did not regret it. He was happy to have turned the page and to be starting all over again. A whole new future stretched out before him, rooted in the deeper memories of his childhood and youth.

The Jesuit, who had picked up a smattering of the language as a prisoner, was duly impressed. He understood bits and pieces of the young man's speech. He liked to think of Radisson as his protégé now that he had brought him back to the Catholic faith and given him access once more to eternal salvation. Poncet could see that Radisson knew every aspect of Iroquois culture and could prove very helpful indeed to the Jesuit priests whose plans had thus far been thwarted by this implacable nation. For his part, Radisson could see that Governor Orlaer was right. Father Poncet could help him make his way back to Paris, perhaps even back to New France, if he went about things the right way.

The two men were made for each other.

The next morning at first light, Orlaer and his lieutenant led the two Frenchmen as discreetly as possible to the boat that would carry them to Manhattan. The captain ordered two beds set up for them in the hold, amid sixty barrels of gunpowder that the boat was to deliver to the capital of the colony. Radisson recognized the same barrels he and his Iroquois had admired at Fort Orange. Peter Orlaer forbade them from leaving their hideout for three days and implored them to be careful not to ignite the powder: the explosion would surely blow up the entire boat and take all passengers with it. Lastly, he gave them each a letter, to be given to the captain of the vessel that would take them on to Holland.

On that cold morning of December 1653, it was time to go. A new life was about to begin for Radisson.